KT-119-833

RELATIVE
PARTNERS

Jeanne Whitmee

CHIVERS LARGE PRINT
BATH

British Library Cataloguing in Publication Data available

This Large Print edition published by Chivers Press, Bath, 1999.

Published by arrangement with the author.

U.K. Hardcover ISBN 0 7540 3785 1
U.K. Softcover   ISBN 0 7540 3786 X

Copyright © Jeanne Whitmee 1987

All rights reserved.

009031
MORAY COUNCIL
LIBRARIES &
INFORMATION SERVICES
F

Printed and bound in Great Britain by
Redwood Books, Trowbridge, Wiltshire

CHAPTER ONE

'When Mr Scott arrives you can show him straight in here, Sandra.'

As the girl nodded and withdrew Danielle looked once more round the office, her eyes anxiously checking every small detail. Yes, everything seemed to be in order. She sat down at her father's desk and tried to calm her fluttering nerves. The whole hotel was in a whirl this morning and she had tried so hard to present a calm outward appearance to the staff that already she felt limp and exhausted with the strain.

What would he be like, this Adam Scott, who was about to cut a swathe through all their lives? She took a deep breath, reminding herself for the hundredth time that it was for the best—and that, anyway, she would be married and away from here before the changes took place.

Restless, she got up and moved across the room to check her appearance in the gilt mirror over the fireplace. Wide grey-green eyes looked back at her out of the small, pale face and she hoped that Adam Scott would not see the apprehension lurking in their depths. She twisted the solitaire engagement ring on her finger. John had wanted to be with her for this first interview with Adam Scott but she

1

had refused. She owed it to her late father to do this last thing for him on her own and with as much dignity as possible.

Once more she wondered how her father could have let the finances of The Royalty Hotel get into such a mess. Until his death two months ago she had had no inkling of the financial collapse facing the business. She still couldn't understand it. Ever since she had left school four years ago she had helped her father run the place, taking charge of the hotel and restaurant bookings and the reception desk; supervising the staff. She had been under the impression that they were doing well. There was hardly a week when they weren't full, especially in the season. Americans especially seemed to like their rather old-fashioned way of doing things and they had a regular clientele who came back time after time to enjoy the gourmet food and relaxed surroundings.

She smoothed the skirt of her neat grey suit and walked to the window. The view was one that never failed to delight her and now, with spring stirring the countryside, it was at its best. The rolling, leafy Cotswold landscape was the perfect setting for The Royalty, once a Tudor manorhouse.

Her father's office was on the first floor, at the front of the house. He had always liked to keep an eye on the drive and watch guests arriving. As she stood there, looking down onto the tree-lined drive, a long, expensive-looking car came into view round the curve and her heart gave a jerk. The car came to a stop under the window where she stood, and she watched as a man got out. He was tall, but the top of his dark head was all she could see from here. It must be Adam Scott. As he reached into the car for a briefcase she took a deep breath and braced herself wishing, just for a fleeting moment that she had agreed to John's being with her. This man looked so assured, so experienced. A business tycoon who ran a chain of luxury hotels must be, while she knew not even enough to save the business that was also the only home she had ever known!

She seated herself at the desk, straightening her back and hoping she looked more confident than she felt; fixing her eyes on the door through which he would come in a few moments. She hoped he would be kind and understanding, but she doubted it.

'Mr Scott, Miss Denver.'

He walked into the room, tall and impeccably dressed in a dark grey suit; seeming to fill the small office with his presence. She rose to meet him, offering her hand, hoping he wouldn't notice how much it trembled.

'How do you do, Mr Scott?'

Sandra withdrew, closing the door quietly behind her.

'Adam, please. After all, we are almost

3

related.'

She was slightly taken aback at the small concession. Dark brown eyes smiled down at her and the hand that gripped hers was warm and firm. But shrewdness hid behind his smile as he took in her trim appearance. Small, pale face framed by auburn curls, large, grey-green eyes that tried to smile through their obvious apprehension. Travelling downwards they saw a trim figure, neatly dressed, slim legs and small feet in high-heeled black shoes. He saw the pale cheeks colour slightly under his scrutiny. She gently disengaged her hand and stepped back behind the mahogany desk as though feeling the necessity to put a barrier between them.

'Please—have a seat—Adam.' She indicated the chair opposite. 'As you know, my name is Danielle, though most people call me Danny.'

He nodded, unzipping his briefcase in a way she thought dismissive. He had made a token gesture of friendliness, now he wanted to get down to business—waste no more time. As she watched the strong hands arranging the papers before him on the desk, she wondered briefly how old he was, guessing at the early thirties. Younger than John by perhaps seven or eight years. There was a sprinkling of silver in the smoothly brushed dark hair, she noticed, and a deeply etched line between the thick eyebrows—as though he frowned a lot. She waited edgily while he studied the papers

taken from the briefcase. When he looked up at her again his expression was grave.

'What a pity we couldn't have met under happier circumstances.'

She nodded, wishing she could think of something intelligent to say. He went on:

'I'm sorry you had a little trouble contacting my stepfather. As I think you know, he is now in semi-retirement and lives a great deal of his time abroad. He is happy to leave the running of the company to me.'

'Oh—I see.' Her heart sank. It was years since Matthew Denver had quarrelled with his brother, James, but when her father had died without leaving a will she had been forced to get in touch with her uncle. She had hoped to deal with him direct and not this stranger, this stepson of his who hadn't even the remotest family link with her. His eyes returned to the papers.

'Well, I need hardly tell you that the books are in the most abysmal mess,' he told her. 'The place appears to have been running at a loss for several years.' He looked up at her. 'Your father must have been using up his capital at an alarming rate. You had no idea of this?'

She shook her head, wondering why she should feel so guilty about it. 'None at all. I only ran the bookings and reception, you see. Daddy—my father—had always managed the financial side of things.'

He raised his eyebrows. 'In this case the

5

word *managed* seems rather a euphemism, if you'll forgive me for saying so!' He drew out a letter. 'I have a letter here from your accountant, John Peterson.'

'My fiance,' she put in. 'We are to be married soon.'

He went on, completely ignoring her remark. 'He tells me that there are quite a number of outstanding debts.'

'I—er—yes. But there is enough money to pay them—isn't there?' Danielle asked anxiously. It seemed she had been right to be nervous. It was turning out to be even worse than she had anticipated. Inwardly she flinched as a flicker of impatience crossed his face, deepening the line between the eyebrows. Clearly, her attempt at appearing calm and assured had failed miserably.

'The question is this, Danielle. Do you wish the business to go into liquidation, or do you want it to be taken over by us—the Denver Group?'

'Oh. To be taken over—I think.' She looked at him across the desk. He was still waiting. She cleared her throat. She must try to sound more positive. *What was it about this man that made her feel so weak and vulnerable?* 'Yes,' she said as firmly as she could. 'To be taken over—definitely.' John had advised her that this was the best course to take. If her uncle decided that The Royalty had potential he would presumably buy her out, whereas, if she went

6

into voluntary bankruptcy she might well come out of it with nothing.

'Good.' He zipped up the briefcase smartly. 'As long as you know what you really want. Of course that will be subject to my examination of the premises,' he told her. 'I have to assess its potential. I take it there will be a room for me here? It may take several days.'

'Oh! Will it?' She had expected it to be a flying visit.

He frowned. 'Is something wrong? Is the hotel full?'

'Oh no!' She smiled, hoping he hadn't picked up the note of dismay in her voice.

'I'm sorry to have to put you to this inconvenience,' he said tartly. 'But you understand that a company like the Denver Group has a reputation to keep up. Only the most . . .'

'It isn't in the *least* inconvenient,' she interrupted, rising from behind the desk. Suddenly her pride reared up. The tone of his remark had stung her. From what she had seen of Denver Hotels they couldn't hold a candle to The Royalty. To her way of thinking the food was far inferior and the service was impersonal. She was damned if she was going to be pushed around by Adam Scott, even if he was here to represent the almighty Denver Group! She pressed the bell by the fireplace. 'I shall have a room prepared for you at once.'

'Thank you.' He stood up. 'I hope you will

7

be free to accompany me on my investigations.' He looked down at her. 'Clearly it would save a great deal of time if you were there to answer my questions.'

She nodded. 'I shall do my best to be available.' She glanced at her watch. 'It is almost lunch time. Will you eat in the restaurant?'

'That would be very pleasant.' He bestowed his flashing smile on her again. 'I hope you will join me?'

'I have an appointment with my fiance,' she told him, not without some satisfaction. 'But if you tell me what time you wish to begin work I shall make it my business to be back.'

John arrived on the dot of one o'clock and took her to lunch in Cirencester. He watched her as she picked at her food; his blue eyes concerned behind the gold-rimmed glasses.

'There's no need for you to worry, you know,' he told her. 'If the Denver Group decide they don't want the place we can always try to find another buyer.'

She glanced up from her chicken salad, her eyes full of doubt. 'But I thought you said this was the only way, with the business in the state it's in?'

'It doesn't have to be sold as a business. Maybe some wealthy Arab would buy it for a country retreat,' he offered hopefully. 'Then you'd be able to pay everything off without calling in the Receiver.'

8

She knew he was only trying to cheer her up. Both of them knew that there was very little hope of a miracle happening now and it would take a miracle to save The Royalty. But Danielle's mind was still reliving the morning's interview with Adam Scott, her resentment growing by the minute.

'You should have heard him,' she complained. 'Talking about the place as though it were a tenth-rate boarding house. It's a far better hotel than those—those glass and concrete monstrosities of theirs!'

'Those glass and concrete monstrosities as you call them are making James Denver and his company a fortune,' he pointed out gently. 'If Adam Scott thinks something can be made of The Royalty just let him get on with it. We'll be married soon anyway.'

'It was my home though,' she told him. 'The only one I've ever known. And another thing—I don't like the implication that Daddy was some kind of bumbling idiot.' Her throat constricted, thickening her voice and John reached across the table to cover her hand with his.

'No one is saying that, Danny. Why not try to give up gracefully? You'll have a new home soon. There'll be a lot to do getting it ready. Why not just concentrate on that?'

After the wedding she and John were to move into the home he had shared with his parents; a three-storeyed Edwardian house on

9

the outskirts of Cirencester. John had said she could have a complete carte blanche in redecorating it but somehow her heart wasn't in it. The place depressed her with its dark brown paintwork and rooms full of heavy, ornate furniture, but she hadn't the heart to tell him.

'I suppose you're right,' she said doubtfully, looking at her watch. 'I'm sorry, John. I shall have to get back now. I promised his lordship I'd be there to give him a conducted tour this afternoon at two precisely.'

He smiled indulgently, taking her keenness as a good sign. He patted her hand. 'That's a good girl. Better not be late.'

Outside in the car he slipped an arm around her shoulders. 'I'll be glad when you're away from The Royalty, Danny. Once we're married you'll soon forget it with all there'll be to interest you.'

Danielle had a brief vision of herself in the vast dark house, giving bridge parties and chairing various committees and her heart sank. She really would have to talk to John— to tell him she wanted to find another job and not live the kind of existence he seemed to envisage for her. She had loved her job at The Royalty and she hoped to find another, similar one when she was forced to leave. But this wasn't the moment to bring it up. There was far too much to think about at the moment.

She had known John since childhood. He

was the son of her father's oldest friend and when Matthew Denver had died so suddenly, leaving his affairs in complete disorder, he had seemed the obvious person to turn to. During that terrible time he had been a tower of strength to her, taking everything out of her hands. It had been John who had found the hotel's books in such a muddle and over the weeks she had come to depend heavily on his strength and wisdom. When he asked her to marry him it had come as no surprise and she had said yes almost without thinking. He had become a necessary part of her life and she had come to depend on him so much that it seemed natural somehow.

During the drive back to Kingswood she was silent. The countryside was so beautiful in the spring sunshine. It was almost symbolic. She had come through the long hard winter and now, at last, it seemed that there was light and hope at the end of the tunnel—if only she didn't have to leave this place she loved so much.

John drew up outside the front entrance of The Royalty and looked at her.

'Sure you're all right, darling?'

She nodded. 'I will be, once all this is over.'

'I'll come and take you to dinner this evening,' he said.

She shook her head. 'I think I'd better be on hand while Adam Scott is here,' she told him. 'I'll ring you with a progress report—keep you

11

in the picture.'

'Just as you think.' He bent to kiss her, but as they drew apart she noticed Adam Scott standing watching them from the hotel entrance. She flushed angrily.

'Honestly! Of all the cheek!'

John followed her glance. 'Is that Scott? I might as well make myself known while I'm here.'

Before she could do anything about it he had got out of the car and was walking towards the other man. Danielle followed reluctantly. By the time she joined them they had introduced themselves. John's five foot ten looked positively short beside Adam's towering height. He had changed into a tweed jacket and well-cut slacks. His hair had a slight wave, she noticed, and it was only the wings brushed back at the sides that were streaked with silver. She watched his shrewd brown eyes assessing John in the same way that he had summed her up, taking in the lean bespectacled face and light brown hair; the slight build and manicured hands. In his business he was clearly accustomed to making snap judgments about people. She found herself wondering what he had thought of her—and surprised herself by wondering if he had found her attractive.

John seemed to be finding him agreeable. He was smiling as she came up to them.

'Well, darling, I'm sure you have a busy

afternoon ahead of you.' He looked at his watch. 'And I have an appointment at two-thirty. I'll ring you tonight.' He kissed her, holding her for just a fraction too long. Once more she found herself flushing under Adam Scott's candid gaze. Was his smile one of indulgence or was he laughing at them?

As John drove away she turned to him. 'Well, shall we make a start?' she said briskly. 'Perhaps you'd like to see outside while it's fine?'

The Royalty stood in ten acres of parkland which Danielle toured with him in the Landrover.

'I notice that your staff seem either very young or quite elderly,' he observed as they drove.

'That is because we have always trained our own staff,' she explained. 'We start them straight from school and many of them stay with us until retirement. Some have been here for as long as I can remember.'

'Mmm, I can well believe that,' he said with a hint of irony.

She gave him a swift glance but his expression told her nothing. 'I hope you enjoyed your lunch.'

'It was very good,' he said. 'I was quite agreeably surprised.'

His patronising tone almost stung her into making a tart remark, but she bit it back. 'Our chef, Arthur Brown, has been with us for a

13

long time,' she told him. 'He trained under one of the finest chefs in the country and once worked at The Savoy.'

He looked at her with raised eyebrows. 'Really? I wonder what went wrong?'

She turned to glare at him, annoyed by the sarcastic edge his voice had assumed. 'Sorry?'

He shrugged. 'Well, I'm sure that even you will agree that The Royalty is hardly the next step *up* from The Savoy. Something must have gone badly wrong for him somewhere.'

'If it did I think you will agree it was our gain,' she told him with a slight shake of her shoulders.

They had arrived beside the small, picturesque lake and she drew up and switched off the engine. It was no accident that she had brought him here first. At this time of year it looked particularly beautiful with the willows that fringed it coming into delicate leaf. Danielle was very proud of the lake. 'Perhaps you might like to get out and walk for a while,' she suggested. 'I think you would see more that way.'

He scanned the surroundings and pointed to a small stone building in the distance. 'What is that?'

'It's a tithe barn,' she told him proudly. 'It's medieval.'

'I see. What do you use it for?'

'*Use* it?' She looked at him indignantly. 'I told you, it's a tithe barn—an ancient

14

monument.'

'But it shouldn't go to waste, surely?' He began to stride in the direction of the barn, Danielle almost running to keep up with him. 'Have you ever considered the idea of using it for medieval banquets?' he asked. She stared at him in horror. He *had* to be joking, surely? But one look at his face told her that he was serious.

'I doubt very much if you'd ever be allowed to do that!' she said.

He smiled. 'Oh, I think the Denver Group might find a way.'

They spent some time exploring the old building with its crumbling walls. Adam was full of ideas, most of which filled Danielle with horror. She couldn't help saying so once or twice. Finally Adam looked at her, his dark eyes flashing.

'I find your attitude obstructive to say the least; short-sighted too,' he told her with brutal frankness. 'It tells me a great deal about the failure of the business. If you want to be successful you must make the best use of every asset. You of all people are in no position to indulge in such high ideals.'

His words stung her into an acid silence. Every instinct she possessed urged her to tell him to go to hell but knew she could afford no such luxury. She would be foolish to throw away the chance of coming out of the deal with money in the bank, just for the sake of satisfying her pride.

'I take it you'll be glad to get out of the hotel business,' he said as they walked back towards the lake.

'Not at all! I've always loved living and working here,' she told him warmly. 'I'm hoping to find another, similar job.'

He looked at her with raised eyebrows. 'You surprise me. I would have thought your fiance the type who liked his little woman safely behind the kitchen door!'

'John isn't in the least like that!' Danielle lied.

He laughed softly, churning up her impotent fury once again. 'What are your plans then, supposing we do decide to buy you out?'

She glanced at him sideways, then took a chance and plunged. The idea she had been nursing had never taken shape except in her own mind. 'What I'd like . . .' she began. 'What I'd *really* like is to stay here and manage The Royalty.'

He stopped in his tracks and looked at her. 'Really? You do surprise me. And what qualifications have you for the job?'

She stared at him. 'I've lived here all my life. The only job I've ever had was here.'

He waved a hand dismissively. 'I realise that, of course. But what training did you have for it?'

'I—I took a secretarial course—and Daddy

16

taught me all he knew ...' she stopped, realising that Adam Scott would hardly consider that to be the perfect groundwork.

He nodded. 'Ah—yes. Well, to work as a manageress for the Denver Group you would be required to start from the bottom,' he told her. 'That means from the kitchens up. We insist on our managers knowing every branch of the business.'

She stared at him indignantly, her cheeks pink. 'You'd expect me to work in the kitchen? Is that what *you* did?'

His expression didn't change as he answered: 'Most certainly. I was eighteen when my mother married your Uncle James. After taking a degree in business management I went straight into the kitchens as a vegetable chef.'

Chastened, she turned away, a lump rising in her throat at the hopelessness of it all. John would certainly never agree to any wife of his working as a kitchen maid!

Suddenly his arm dropped over her shoulders. 'Don't look so despondent, Danielle,' he said, as though reading her mind. 'I'm sure your husband will find plenty to occupy you—that is if you ever actually marry him!'

CHAPTER TWO

'Oh, Arthur, what on earth am I going to do?' Danielle wailed. She was curled up in the basket chair by the window of Arthur Brown's comfortable, shabby sitting room. He had a small flat under the eaves of The Royalty and ever since she could remember Danielle had retreated here in times of stress.

Arthur was sixty, tall and spare with thinning grey hair and kindly blue eyes that could twinkle wickedly with a quirky humour that was all his own. He had been chef at The Royalty since before Danielle was born and after her mother died ten years ago he had taken on the role of nursemaid cum father confessor.

'Surely it can't be as bad as you think.' He handed her a steaming mug of tea. 'After all, your uncle promised we'd all keep our jobs, didn't he?'

'Oh yes. I insisted on that,' Danielle told him. 'Maybe I won't be here, but I wanted to make sure that none of you suffered.'

'So what's troubling you so badly?' Arthur sat down opposite her, giving her his lovable lop-sided grin. 'Tell old Arthur what it's all about, eh?'

Danielle took a long drink of the strong, comforting tea and looked at him over the rim

18

of the mug. 'I love this place,' she told him with a catch in her voice. 'And that man is going to turn it into a—a *hamburger bar*!'

Arthur laughed. 'Not while I'm here, he isn't! Anyway, you're exaggerating, surely?'

She shook her head. 'I'm not. You should have heard what he had in mind for the tithe barn—Medieval banquets, would you believe?'

Arthur looked thoughtful. 'Now *that's* not a bad idea, you know. Not a bad idea at all.'

She stared at him. '*Arthur!* You can't be serious!'

'Ah, but I am,' he told her. 'Properly done, they'd be a great draw. Of course they'd have to be properly researched and done authentically. And it might be tricky getting permission, but all the same . . .' He got up and went over to a shelf of books. 'Somewhere here I've got a book on Elizabethan food—ah—here it is.'

Danielle watched wistfully as he delved into the book. 'I want to stay here, Arthur,' she told him quietly. 'If there are new things happening at The Royalty I want to be part of it. I want to have some say in what changes are made and share in the excitement.'

The chef put down his book and looked shrewdly at her. 'Oh, dear. That's what's at the bottom of all this, isn't it?' He resumed his seat opposite and took both her hands in his. 'Why don't you just tell this Adam Scott that you'd like to stay on?' he asked.

'I did,' she told him. 'He said that to become a Denver Group manageress I'd have to start training all over again—from the kitchen upward.'

Arthur smiled. 'He's putting you on, surely?'

Danielle snorted. 'Not on your life! Apparently he did it himself, damn him!'

Arthur sighed. 'Well that *is* the way it's done, love. But I'd have thought in your case . . .' He left the sentence unfinished and gave her his warm smile. 'Never mind. You'd be training under me. That wouldn't be so bad now, would it?'

'It's not that *I'd* mind. It's John,' she told him doubtfully. 'I can't see him taking kindly to the idea at all.'

Arthur's face clouded. 'Have you discussed it with him?'

She shook her head. 'That's just it. He's taking it for granted that I'll take over the running of Langworth House—sit on committees and give little bridge parties, just like his mother did. I know he doesn't see me as a working wife at all.'

'You're going to have to sort it out with him. I think you know that, don't you?' Arthur looked at her with concern.

'Oh, I will—sometime,' Danielle shrugged impatiently. She was all too aware that she was shelving the problem and being reminded of the fact didn't help. 'Just at the moment all I can think about is proving to Adam Scott that

The Royalty can't—*mustn't*, be turned into some kind of fast-food joint. I admit that Daddy must have slipped up badly financially, but I'm convinced our way is still best—at least, for this place.' She bit her lip. 'Oh—I could *kill* Adam Scott! He's so brash. So sure that he's right.'

Arthur squeezed her hands warmly. 'Now, calm down. Getting worked up never achieves anything, I'm always telling you that. And you know, you have everything that's needed to put your case without lifting a finger, if you think about it.'

She looked up at him. 'How?'

'He's a man, isn't he?' Arthur gave her his wicked grin. 'You can charm the birds out of the trees when you've a mind to, Danny Denver. Just use your feminine wiles on him. If he doesn't come round to your way of thinking I'll eat my hat!'

Danielle pulled a wry face. 'But I don't even *like* him. He's so sure of himself, so self-opinionated and conceited.'

'He's a handsome fellow though, and not averse to a little feminine flattery, I'll bet.' Arthur leaned forward. 'I take it you'll be having dinner with him here this evening?'

She nodded, giving him a baleful look. 'I'm dreading it!'

'Then don't! Look forward to it instead. Put on your best frock and make yourself look beautiful. I'll lay on one of my special dinners.'

Arthur half-closed his eyes thoughtfully. 'And let me see—yes, I suggest you invite him to join you in the Cavalier Room.'

Danielle suddenly sat up straight and looked at him, unable to hide a smile in spite of her anxiety. 'Arthur Brown! What *are* you suggesting?'

The Cavalier Room was a small, private room used for intimate occasions such as anniversary dinners. It could take three tables but more often than not was booked for candlelight dinners for two. The staff referred to it as the 'seduction suite'.

Arthur laughed. 'I'm suggesting that you get him to relax, that's all. Be as wittily feminine and entertaining as only you can. Tell him about your own ideas for The Royalty. Put it across with your own natural charm and I'm sure he'll be sympathetic. It'll certainly work better than handing him the frozen lemon treatment. I guarantee it!'

Danielle considered the suggestion for a moment but once again resentment soured her thoughts. Just how far was she supposed to go in the name of duty? Good looking Adam Scott might be but everything about him fought with her own ideas and beliefs. 'You're asking a lot,' she grumbled. 'Do you know what he had the nerve to say to me this afternoon?' When Arthur shook his head she continued: 'I was talking about John and he actually had the nerve to voice doubts about

22

our suitability for one another!'

Arthur was silent for a moment. Clearly Adam Scott had a cheek to pass such an opinion on such short acquaintance, but he could not deny that he had had similar doubts about Danielle's choice of husband. Scott was obviously an intensely shrewd man. Perhaps he wouldn't be so easily won over after all. He looked up to find the girl staring at him.

'Arthur—did you hear what I said?'

'I did. And of course you're right to be annoyed,' he told her. 'Your personal life is none of his business. However, I do think that if you want your own way over this you're going to have to pocket your pride and ignore his observations.' He smiled at her hopefully. 'Now, I'll get my notebook and we'll work out a menu for tonight, shall we? The most seductive food we can dream up!'

She sighed resignedly. 'All right. I'll try it your way. But don't expect me to enjoy it!'

After Danielle had taken Adam Scott for a tour of the hotel grounds in the Landrover that afternoon he had assured her that he could find his own way. He wanted to explore thoroughly by himself, he told her, familiarise himself with the geography of the place, leaving the business side of things until the following day. That was when she had left him and sought out Arthur.

The remark about John had disturbed her deeply. More deeply than she had confessed,

23

even to Arthur. It had been so casually delivered that at first she had wondered if she had heard correctly and now, as she made her way back to the office, she went back over the conversation again.

'I'm sure your husband will find plenty to occupy you—that is if you ever actually *marry* him.'

He had said it so smoothly, one arm draped across her shoulders. For a moment she had been stunned into silence.

'Of *course* I'm going to marry him.' She turned to look up at him. 'We're engaged!'

He'd laughed, a deep-throated chuckle. 'No need to look so indignant. After all, there's many a slip as they say.'

She felt her cheeks colouring as she protested warmly. 'John is a wonderful person. There'll be no slip between us.' She shrugged off his arm. 'We're getting married just as soon as everything is settled here and I have Daddy's affairs sorted out.' Thinking about it now, she must have sounded very much on the defensive. Perhaps she had only confirmed his opinion.

'Congratulations!' he had said. 'As long as you really know what you're doing I'm sure you'll be very happy.'

There she should have left it but she couldn't. She had to know what he had meant by the oblique remark, so she pressed on, her voice edgy and sharp; 'Of course I know what

I'm doing. And anyway, what makes you say that there's many a slip?'

He sighed, looking bored suddenly. 'I'm sorry if it offended you. Please forget it. It's just that from the little I saw he seemed a little—what shall I say—mature, for you—both in years *and* manner.' He turned to look straight into her eyes. 'A young woman who has just lost her father must be rather vulnerable, I imagine.'

She stared at him, hardly able to believe her ears. How dared he suggest that she was looking for a father figure in John? She had opened her mouth to protest hotly, then thought better of it. Deep inside perhaps she was a little afraid that if she pursued the question further she would be opening a Pandora's Box containing all her own doubts and fears, so far comfortably submerged. Quickening her walk in the direction of the Landrover she had said crisply: 'I shall be busy for the rest of the afternoon, Mr Scott, so I'll leave you to look around. Please feel free to go anywhere you like. If there's anything you want to know—about the *business*—I'll be available from five o'clock onwards.' But she hadn't quite been able to keep her voice from trembling and when she turned to look at him she had been put out to see that he was smiling. The significance of her stress on the word *business* hadn't escaped his notice. She had got the message across.

25

He gave her a courtly bow. 'Thank you for your cooperation—Miss Denver. I shall try not to take up too much of your valuable time. Perhaps we might have dinner together this evening? That is if your fiance doesn't have a prior claim on you.'

She had ignored his mocking gesture and the cynicism of the remark as she climbed into the Landrover and switched on the engine. 'That will be quite convenient. I'll let you know what time.'

After she left Arthur's room, Danielle went back to the office and rang for Sandra whom she despatched with a message to Adam Scott saying that they would dine in the Cavalier Room but that she would meet him in the bar at seven. She thought the girl looked at her oddly but she dismissed the notion. She was getting over-sensitive, she told herself. It was that man. Even thinking about him seemed to bring out the worst in her. She really must pull herself together and behave like a mature woman instead of a silly schoolgirl, forever on the defensive. In essence Arthur was quite right. So far she had handled the situation in a stupidly immature way.

She turned her attention to signing the letters that Maggie Jones, her father's part-time secretary, had typed during her absence. Maggie had gone home, but she had left a message that a pressing letter had been received by the second post from the wine merchants regarding an unpaid bill. Danielle picked it up and sighed despairingly when she saw the amount outstanding. Something must be done—and done fast. This evening she would have to pull out all the stops to prove to Adam that she was prepared to cooperate after all.

In her room she opened her wardrobe and looked through her collection of dresses. She guessed that Adam was the type of man who would dress formally—if not a dinner jacket he would wear a dark suit. She would match his formality. Reaching to the back of the wardrobe she took out a simple, slim-fitting black chiffon dress. It was cut low at the neckline with thin shoestring straps at the shoulders. The skirt fitted smoothly over the waist to flare out below, swirling romantically about her hips. She held it against herself, nodding with satisfaction, then laid it carefully across the bed before going off to shower.

At seven she was ready and stood before the mirror surveying herself critically. With the starkly plain dress she wore the single diamond on a cobweb-fine chain that her father had given her for her twenty-first birthday. It flashed against her ivory skin, reflecting the fire in her eyes as she prepared herself mentally for the evening ahead. Adam Scott was obviously used to a more mature, sophisticated type of woman. She must try to show him that she wasn't the naive little idiot he seemed to think her. She would show him that even his first impression could be wrong. At least she hoped she would!

She had made up her face with the utmost care. Wide green eyes fringed by sweeping dark lashes looked back luminously at her from the mirror. Her delicate cheekbones were emphasised by a natural pink flush and her skin glowed like pale satin. She had secured her bright hair up into a curly topknot from which small tendrils escaped to soften the severity of the line. She held up a hand mirror, turning this way and that, hoping she looked sophisticated. Looking at her watch she saw that it was almost ten past seven; she had kept him waiting just long enough, she assessed, to whet his appetite without seeming rude.

He was waiting in the bar, sitting on one of the high stools and looking relaxed as he chatted to Bill, her chief barman. She had guessed right about the suit. It was dark grey with a faint pin-stripe, perfectly tailored, fitting smoothly over the broad shoulders and slim hips, the white shirt he wore with it complementing the tan that spoke of travel in warmer climes. His dark hair gleamed under the subdued lighting of the bar. She stood unobserved in the doorway for a few moments, watching. Bill was laughing. He seemed totally at ease with Adam as did the other members of the staff. He had a way of making them relax—gaining their confidence and no doubt finding out all he wanted to know, she thought wryly. Well, maybe if she played her cards right she could match him at his own game!

He turned and saw her. Getting off his stool he came towards her, his eyes sweeping over her with an open admiration that heightened her colour.

'I'm sorry, I think I'm a little late,' she said coolly.

The dark eyebrows rose. 'Are you?' He looked at his watch. 'I hadn't noticed, but I'm sure the time was well spent. You look quite lovely. I'm flattered.' He put a hand under her elbow and led her to the bar. 'What will you have to drink? I think something special is called for under the circumstances.'

'Please ...' She laid a hand on his arm. 'While you are here you are my guest.' She looked at the barman. 'We'll have two dry Martinis, please, Bill and will you put a bottle of champagne on ice for us?'

The barman smiled. 'I already have, Miss Denver. Arthur's orders.'

Adam looked impressed. 'I see you have your staff well trained!' When Bill had moved off to attend to two other customers Adam looked at her with a shake of his head. 'It's a nice gesture, Danielle, but we both know that you can't afford hospitality of this kind. You must let me pay just as I would in any other hotel.'

She flushed and looked away, playing with the stem of her glass. Damn him! Couldn't he allow her even that small gesture of independence? 'You might allow me just one little concession,' she told him quietly. She turned to look at him. 'It's humiliating, going broke, you know.'

He smiled back into her eyes, and laid a hand lightly on her arm. 'If it means that much to you I'll give in gracefully. Thank you.'

The touch of his hand was light, but Danielle drew her arm away involuntarily, shaken by the electric tingle his touch aroused. Her heart sank. This evening could be even more of an ordeal than she had anticipated.

The Cavalier Room was furnished in Jacobean style, with heavy wine-coloured velvet curtains and dark oak furniture. A wood fire crackled in the stone fireplace, giving off an aromatic fragrance and tall red candles flickered in their silver sticks on an impeccably-laid table. Adam took it all in with obvious appreciation.

'Well, this is delightful.' He settled Danielle into her seat and took his own seat opposite in the high-backed chair. Mark, the head waiter, served them with their first course, moving quietly and withdrawing to leave them alone. Adam tasted his smoked salmon and looked up at Danielle.

'Delicious.'

As the meal progressed he expressed his

approval and Danielle felt herself relaxing for the first time that day. Good food and wine uncoiled the tension within her and to her surprise she found herself beginning to enjoy the evening. Over the main course, chicken in Arthur's own special white wine sauce, she looked up at Adam.

'I suppose I shouldn't ask, but have you come to any conclusions yet?'

He looked across the table at her, his eyes warm. 'About what?'

She blushed. 'About The Royalty, of course.'

'Ah . . .' he smiled. 'Well, I've only taken an informal look today, as I told you, but already I can see where your father's methods were uneconomical.' He held up his hand. 'Not that the service here isn't impeccable—it is. It's just that he was charging too little for what he was giving.' He picked up a spoon. 'Crested plate, for instance. I'll bet quite a few of these found their way into suitcases as "souvenirs". Stainless steel does the same job and it doesn't need cleaning.' He touched the damask tablecloth. 'I find that laundry is done on the premises too—and no wonder with linen like this. There are perfectly good hotel linen services, you know. Another big saving on costs.'

Danielle shook her head stubbornly. 'The Royalty has a name for these touches. Daddy was always very proud of that. Besides, we are about the only source of employment in this village.'

'But you're a hotel proprietor, my dear, not the local lady bountiful. I haven't actually been through the books yet, but I suspect I could find a dozen ways to cut costs in as many minutes.'

Danielle put down her fork, her appetite for Arthur's delicious food fading. 'I wish I hadn't asked.'

He reached across the table to touch her hand. 'We won't speak about it again this evening. Please, eat your dinner. It's much too good to waste. We'll talk about something else. Tell me the history of this house—and how it got its name.'

She was tempted to let him see her displeasure by making some tart remark, but she swallowed her pride, remembering Arthur's advice, and launched into a brief history of the house, soon finding herself warming to what had always been her favourite subject. She recounted to him the house's Civil War connections and the romantic legends associated with the place. Once she caught sight of herself in the gilt mirror over the fireplace. Her cheeks were pink and her eyes were sparkling. The wood fire, the champagne and good food had brought her to life and released some of her inhibitions; things which Adam was quick to notice and appreciate. Over coffee he asked her suddenly:

'What do you really want to do with your life, Danielle?'

She looked at him, taken off-guard. Hadn't he worked that out for himself by now? 'Best of all I'd like to stay here,' she told him.

'You're young. Wouldn't you like to broaden your horizons—see the world?'

She looked at her plate, suddenly unable to meet his steady gaze. 'That would be nice—if I could come back here afterwards.'

'But you can't—can you?' The dark eyes were almost black as they looked into hers. 'Let's face it, Danielle, even if you were willing to start training all over again, your future husband doesn't look the type to let his wife follow a career. I think you've come to the end of a phase in your life, haven't you?'

She felt her heart contract. Put like that it sounded frighteningly final. 'I suppose I have,' she whispered.

'You must love him very much,' he said quietly. 'This place obviously means a lot to you, yet you're giving it up for him.'

Her eyes were wide as they met his. 'I'm not! I was forced to give it up,' she said quickly. 'I would never if—if . . .' She stopped short, suddenly aware of what he'd tricked her into admitting. She flushed dully and lowered her eyes. 'I don't want to talk about that either, if you don't mind.'

'I'm sorry.' He looked at his watch. 'Look, it's early yet—and a beautiful evening outside.

How about taking a little walk?'

She got to her feet eagerly, grateful for the diversion. 'That would be nice. I'll fetch a coat.'

He was right; it was a beautiful evening. A new moon had risen and the air was still and quiet. Although it was cool there was a hint of spring warmth, the sharp fragrance of freshly-turned earth and new-mown grass in the air. They walked down to the lake, Danielle pointing out some of the old trees that grew in the grounds as they went. Adam was quiet until they reached the water's edge when he suddenly said without looking at her:

'You're throwing your life away. You know that, don't you?'

She turned to stare up at his profile, etched ruggedly against the dusky sky. They had known each other only a few hours and yet he was talking to her like this. He had made his views clear to her, so why couldn't he leave the subject alone? After all, it had nothing to do with his business here. She should have been angry but something about the set of his mouth, the tension in his expression, stopped the retort that rose to her lips.

'Beggars can't be choosers,' she said quietly.

'Lovely ones like you can.' He turned to her. 'Don't tell me you aren't aware of your considerable attraction, Danielle.' He reached out and took her shoulders, pulling her towards him. When his lips came down on hers she was shocked by her own unexpected reaction. It was as though her body took over, leaving her a stunned onlooker. His mouth, hard and demanding at first, softened into sensuous exploration. She found her own lips parting in surrender. She leaned weakly against him as he slipped her coat from her shoulders and let it fall onto the ground as he pulled her closer. His lips left hers and he buried his face in her hair, his hands caressing the bare skin of her back, inflaming her senses and quickening her heartbeat in a way she found almost frightening. She heard herself murmuring—knew she should stop him—if only she had the strength. His mouth claimed hers again and once more she surrendered to the assault on her senses. She felt his fingers deftly unzipping her dress but there was nothing she could do about it. His touch—his closeness overwhelmed her and when his cool fingers touched her bare skin it was as though a million stars were suddenly exploded inside her head. Deep inside, one remaining shred of sanity told her that the next move must come from her.

Feeling her stiffen slightly in his arms he raised his head to look down at her, his eyes burning into hers. 'You're beautiful, Danielle. Shall we go inside now?'

She stared up at him, dazedly. He hadn't exactly *said* 'your room or mine' but the implication was there. His breath was warm on her cheek, and the caressing touch of his hands still stirred all kinds of traitorous responses in her. What was she *thinking* about to let this happen? her mind demanded. She must be mad!

Pushing him away she pulled up the strap of her dress, shaking her head wordlessly as she took a step backwards.

'Danielle?' He reached out for her again, his eyes questioning but she turned in a panic and began to run back towards the house. He caught her easily, grabbing her arm almost roughly and jerking her to a standstill.

'What the hell do you think you're doing?' His voice was ragged, his face dark with anger as he stared down at her. 'What do you think people will say if you go in like that, for heaven's sake?'

She looked down at her dishevelled state and bit her lip. 'I'm sorry,' she gasped breathlessly. 'But you've got the wrong, idea. Maybe it's my fault . . .'

His fingers bit deeply into the flesh of her arm as he glared down at her. '*Your* fault? I'll say it's your fault. And don't tell me I've got the wrong idea! What's the matter, Danielle— cold feet? I'm not a fool, you know. I got the message the moment I saw the candlelight dinner you'd laid on with all the trimmings.'

She shook her head, her mouth dropping open in horror. 'No! It wasn't—I didn't!'

He laughed harshly. 'A little quiet seduction

36

to get your own way? Well all right. I'll go along with that. You can have the job you want here—anything you like, but don't welsh on me, Danielle. That *would* be letting the side down, wouldn't it?'

She knew he was mocking her; letting her know that he saw through her naivety and his words brought tears to her eyes. What an utter fool she was not to have anticipated this. She might have known how it would look. 'You're wrong!' she lashed out at him. 'I realised I'd been short with you since you arrived and I was sorry. I wanted to make amends. I'm not the sort of girl you seem to take me for.'

'Aren't you?' he laughed. Grasping her by the shoulders he pulled her to him again. 'And how do you know what kind of girl I take you for?' His eyes searched hers and he held her close, so close that she could feel the beat of his heart against her own, the hardness of his body against hers. His breath was harsh against her ear as he whispered: 'I'll tell you something, Danielle. You're not in love with the man you're engaged to. But then you don't really need me to tell you that, do you?'

CHAPTER THREE

Danielle slept little that night. Lying in the darkness she burned with shame at the memory of the way she had responded to Adam's kisses. She had behaved so cheaply. She had deserved the bitter things he had said. It must have been the champagne, she told herself. Tossing and turning she wondered why she hadn't seen how it would look—the candlelight meal—champagne and what Arthur had called 'seductive food'. No use blaming the chef. Dear innocent Arthur still thought of her as twelve years old, able to twist the two elderly men in her life round her little finger. Was that her trouble, she asked herself; was she too sheltered, too spoiled and pampered? Was her reason for wanting to remain at The Royalty simply a reaction against growing up—and was it possible that that was also the reason she had agreed to marry John; safe, reliable—predictable John?

'But I *love* him,' she told herself insistently, turning over for the hundredth time. 'When we are married everything will be all right. This time yesterday I didn't have a doubt in my mind and Adam Scott was no more than a name to me!'

But when she closed her eyes it was Adam's face she saw. She felt his lips claiming hers in

38

that stirringly assertive way and recalled the excited beating of her heart as she had capitulated in his arms. Yet to Adam she had merely been an hour's amusement—possibly a one-night-stand. John loved her, so why had she never felt that with him—*why?*

She overslept and cut out breakfast, unable to face the thought of meeting Adam in the dining room. In her office she tackled the mail. More bills. Maggie wouldn't be in until the afternoon, so she must make the more important telephone calls herself and tape some letters before looking at the advance bookings. She stared at the pile of enquiries for the summer season. What should she do about them? With the future of The Royalty so uncertain could she go ahead and make advance bookings? It was something she would have to ask Adam about, like it or not. She was still mulling it over when the house telephone on her desk rang, startling her. She picked up the receiver.

'Good morning. Office.'

'Danielle?'

Adam's voice made her heart turn a somersault. 'Yes.'

'You weren't at breakfast. I wondered if you were all right.'

'I'm fine, thank you.' She managed to keep her voice steady in spite of the sickening throbbing in her chest. 'I'm glad you rang. There are things we must discuss—business

39

matters.'

'I think there are more than business matters to discuss. Are you free now? I was planning to go out in about half an hour.'

'Of course.' She steeled herself. Better get it over with as soon as possible. 'I'll have some coffee sent in.'

She rang through to the kitchen and ordered coffee, which arrived at the same time as Adam. She was glad; clearing a place for the tray on her desk and finding a chair for him gave her something to do with her trembling hands. At last the waitress withdrew and she found herself forced to look at him. He met her eyes without a flicker, looking at her directly.

'First about last night . . .' he began.

She drew in her breath sharply. 'I think the best thing would be to forget it,' she said tightly.

'I agree—as long as you'll accept my apology. I behaved extremely badly.'

She found herself unable to meet his steady gaze. Picking up a paper knife she turned it over and over nervously. 'Not at all. It was naive of me not to have seen the way it was bound to appear.'

There was a small silence, then he said: 'You wanted to see me.'

'Yes.' She cleared her throat, touching the pile of letters on the desk in front of her. 'I've had a number of enquiries for the summer,' she told him. 'I was wondering whether to go ahead and book them or if I should have a standard letter printed.'

He drew a deep breath. 'As a matter of fact I spent half the night drawing up a plan for an idea I've had,' he told her. 'That's why I want to go out. There are some enquiries I need to make and then I have to send a cable to James—to your uncle. As you know, he's in America at the moment.'

'May I ask what the idea is?' she asked.

'Of course. For some time now we've been thinking of opening a chain of conference centres. I'd like The Royalty to be the first,' he told her. 'I'm convinced it would work superbly. It's right in the centre of the country—beautiful, relaxing surroundings and it would adapt ideally.'

She nodded, interested in spite of herself. A conference centre was better than a hamburger joint! 'It sounds like a very interesting idea.' A thought suddenly struck her. 'You *would* keep on all the present staff, wouldn't you? Uncle James gave me that guarantee.'

'Of course. I don't see why not ...' He hesitated. 'With the possible exception of your chef.'

She stared at him. 'Arthur? But you can't dismiss him!' she protested. 'This place is his whole life and besides, he'd never get another job at his age!'

Adam shook his head. 'Those are the kind of sentiments that helped to ruin your father, if you don't mind my saying so.' He held up his hand as she opened her mouth to speak again. 'The kind of food Arthur Brown is used to preparing is hardly suitable for a conference centre. We'd need good plain food, economically prepared to run the place at a profit. That kind of work would bore a chef of his calibre to death in a week. The man's an artist.'

'I'm sure he'll be glad to know how much you appreciate his talents,' Danielle remarked ironically. She leaned forward, changing her tone, her eyes pleading. If she was to save Arthur's job she would have to tackle this with tact. 'Don't sack Arthur. He's like a second father to me. It would break his heart. He'll adapt. I promise you. Surely you can do that one small thing for me?' Suddenly she flushed as she realised how it sounded. He would think she was playing on what happened last night to get her own way.

He looked at her for several seconds without replying, then he got to his feet abruptly. 'All right. I'll talk to him about it, but I'll make no promises.' He turned to her at the door. 'I hope he appreciates what a friend he has in you.' He pointed to the letters on the desk. 'As for those, better have a standard letter done as you suggested. Say the hotel will be closed for alterations.' He looked at her hesitantly for a moment. 'Danielle, I hope you won't mind, but I'll probably be here for some time if your uncle agrees to my plan.'

Her heart sank but she tried hard to keep her expression under control. 'Of course. I understand. If you want a place to work I can arrange another desk for you in here and I'm sure that Maggie, my secretary, would be happy to type any letters for you.'

'That's very thoughtful. Thank you. But I shall be sending for Bobby Hayward, my P.A. Perhaps you could have another room prepared?'

'Of course. I'll attend to it.'

For a moment they looked at each other. There was a flicker of hesitation in his eyes and Danielle was sure he was going to mention the previous evening again. Her heart quickened with apprehension. It was so embarrassing. Nothing either of them said was going to blot the episode out. Much better to be strictly businesslike—pretend it never happened. Adam must have come to the same conclusion. Grasping the handle he pulled the door open, glancing back at her over his shoulder.

'I'd be grateful if you didn't mention any of my ideas to the staff yet. It's still very much in the air and I'd prefer to wait until I get a reaction from your uncle.'

'Naturally.'

'I'll be on my way then. Goodbye.'

'Goodbye.' As the door closed she drew a long breath of relief. The tension had been almost unbearable. It was only after he'd gone that she realised they hadn't touched the coffee.

She poured herself a cup and drank it slowly. The encounter with Adam had left her quite limp. Just how long *would* he be staying, she wondered? She would have to arrange some kind of rota for the office. The thought of working with him in here was impossible.

She worked through the pile of mail and composed the letter Adam had suggested, leaving it on Maggie's desk to be duplicated later and sent out to each one of their regular guests as well as all future enquiries. Perhaps later they should send a notice to all the papers and magazines in which they advertised. Or would Adam perhaps agree to letting the restaurant remain open during the alterations? If it hadn't been for the personal tension between them she would have thought to mention this possibility to him that morning. There was so much to plan and discuss. They would obviously be working together a great deal during the coming weeks. The sooner they got their relationship onto a businesslike level, the better. At least his personal assistant would be here to act as a catalyst between them, thank goodness.

She made the usual tour of the hotel, ending up in the kitchen where she spoke to

Arthur about menus and the ordering of food. The chef looked at her enquiringly.

'Well, how did it go?' he asked. 'Was the dinner a success?'

She gave him a wry smile. 'Your dinner was great, Arthur. I don't know if I handled the situation with as much skill though. But thanks for your effort.'

She went back to the office and dialled John's number. She felt edgy and restless. Perhaps if she were to get away from the place for a few hours—see John and reassure herself about her feelings for him. His familiar voice filled her with relief.

'Danny! So you've surfaced? How are things going?'

'Fine.' She tried to sound cheerful and convincing. 'I wondered if you were free for lunch?'

'Of course. I'll pick you up at one.' Sensing the note of strain in her voice he asked: 'You *are* all right, aren't you?'

'Yes, I told you. I'm fine. It's just . . .'

'Just what?'

'John—could we go somewhere this afternoon? I feel like a break.'

'Well, I did have a client coming in at three—but I'll put him off.'

'You're sure?'

'Of course. If you want a break, then a break you shall have.'

Over lunch she told him about Adam Scott's

plan to turn The Royalty into a conference centre. He nodded his approval.

'I think that's a super idea. I'm sure there isn't one for miles around and I always think a special centre is so much better than holding a conference in a hotel. He'll be wanting to make extensive alterations, no doubt?'

'Yes. I think he plans to stay on for quite a while. He's sending for his P.A.' She twisted the stem of her wine glass. 'There's just one thing that bothers me. He's agreed to keep on all the staff—except Arthur.'

John looked sceptical. 'Well, I can't honestly say I'm surprised, darling. He is getting a bit long in the tooth.'

She stared at him indignantly. 'He's the finest chef in the country and he's perfectly fit. Anyway, it isn't that. Adam is afraid that the work might bore him. I've managed to persuade him to talk it over with Arthur. I just hope they can come to some agreement.'

'Does he know about Arthur's little weakness?' John asked with a wry smile.

Danielle pulled down the corners of her mouth. She had often regretted telling John Arthur's secret. 'Well, no,' she admitted.

'And what if he lets you down? It wouldn't be the first time, would it?'

Danielle coloured as she looked at him. 'Arthur has never let me down. I know he still lapses at times and has a drink or two, but it never affects his work. He's far too professional to let it.'

Many years before, Arthur Brown had had a drink problem. It had been the cause of his losing his job at The Savoy. Danielle's father had taken pity on him, helping him to kick the habit and then giving him a job at The Royalty where he had been ever since.

John shrugged. 'Well, you know best, darling.' He looked at his watch. 'Well, where would you like to go this afternoon?'

Danielle took a deep breath. Over lunch a plan had been slowly forming in her mind, but now that the time had come to put it into action she wasn't so sure. 'I thought we might go to the house,' she said tentatively. 'Perhaps make a few plans.'

John looked surprised and pleased. 'Well, of course, if that's what you'd like. To tell you the truth I've been wondering whether you liked the idea of living at Langworth House; whether perhaps I was being selfish, expecting you to.'

Danielle pictured the large Victorian house with a heavy heart. Obviously she hadn't hidden her feelings about it as well as she had thought. 'Whatever gave you that idea?' She tried to laugh as she got up from the table; forcing a note of enthusiasm into her voice as she added: 'I'm quite looking forward to redecorating—making it ours.'

Langworth House stood on the edge of the town. It had been built on high ground and was reached by driving in through tall wrought-iron gates and along a curved drive bordered by rhododendron bushes and tall conifers. Danielle found the whole effect claustrophobic. The first thing she would do would be to cut them down, she decided; letting in more light and air. When the house came into view she felt the same feeling of depression that she always felt, but today she was determined to try and see the place in a more optimistic light. She tried to ignore the ugliness of the façade, the pretentious little turrets with their spiky railings and the tall, neo-Gothic mullions. At least the windows were large, the ceilings high and the rooms well proportioned.

In the hall the stained glass panels let into the front door cast coloured reflections on the tiled floor. Danielle looked around her. Perhaps a plain fitted carpet—rose pink or moss green. And the hideous ornate hallstand would have to go, along with that creepy elephant's foot umbrella holder.

John opened the door that led to the small sitting room he had made his own. He used only two rooms of the house now that he lived here alone. It was cosier in here, the furniture plainer and more functional—a desk, a settee and a couple of comfortable armchairs. As she walked in through the door a thought suddenly struck Danielle. The prospect of an afternoon alone with one's fiance should be exciting—

48

she should be longing to close the door and fall into his arms—impervious to the surroundings, so why were the only thoughts in her mind concerned with hall stands and fitted carpets? Suddenly she turned impulsively and put her arms around his neck.

'Oh, John, I can't *wait* till we're married!'

He was slightly taken aback. Sometimes lately he had wondered whether she regretted her quick acceptance of his proposal. He kissed her and she clung to him in a way she never had before. When their lips parted she buried her head against his shoulder, slipping her arms around him beneath his jacket and pressing close to him. She raised her face to his and he kissed her again, laughing a little uneasily as he released her.

'*Well!* What brought all this on?'

She shook her head. Why didn't he sweep her off her feet—carry her off and make love to her so that the nagging doubts in the back of her mind would be obliterated once and for all? 'We're engaged, aren't we? Isn't this the way engaged couples are supposed to act?' she asked edgily.

He pulled her close again, his hands on her waist. 'I'm not complaining! Don't get that idea.' He kissed her again, lingeringly, his face flushed as he looked down at her. 'I think we should go now,' he said huskily.

'Why?' she demanded impatiently. Why couldn't he sense her need—see that their relationship hung in the balance?

He took a deep breath. 'Because you're very lovely, Danielle, and if you go on behaving this way I'm going to lose control.'

'And would that be so terrible?' She tried to sound teasing while all the time she could have shaken him.

He shook his head at her, puzzled as he looked into her eyes. Somehow they seemed over-bright this afternoon, something almost akin to desperation in their grey-green depths. 'You're in a strange mood today,' he remarked. 'Are you sure you're feeling all right?'

She gave an exasperated little snort, 'Oh, for heaven's sake! Is it *abnormal* to want to be kissed?' she asked. 'Didn't you guess when I suggested coming here to the house?' She looked into his eyes, winding her arms seductively around his neck again. 'Make love to me, John,' she whispered, her lips close to his ear. 'I—I don't want to wait any longer.'

She felt a shudder go through him as he pressed her close. Unfastening the buttons of her shirt with trembling fingers, he looked down at her, catching his breath as his hand made contact with the warm, firm flesh of her breast.

'You're sure about this—it's what you really want?'

Danielle nodded, closing her eyes as they sank together onto the settee. Under John's

50

caressing hands she waited for the fireworks to explode, for the wings of desire to lift her as they had last night. She had to prove to herself that it was different with John—different and *better*. It *had* to be! If it wasn't . . . She waited, willing herself to respond, urging her body to tingle, her senses catch fire, but all in vain.

John's breathing was heavy, his breath hot against her neck as he murmured soft endearments. She couldn't stop him now. It would be too cruel after she herself had been the instigator. If only she could feel something. What had happened to make her so frigid? Until yesterday she had always enjoyed John's kisses.

She closed her eyes, waiting for what now seemed inevitable. Perhaps afterwards she would feel a deeper commitment—perhaps it would take time for the magic to work.

Somewhere in the house a door slammed and John swore softly, raising his head to stare down at her, his face startled.

'Damn! I'd forgotten. It's Mrs Downs, my cleaning woman. This is her afternoon.'

Danielle stared at him, feeling a sense of humiliation as she watched him move guiltily away from her. It was made worse when he said:

'Quick, slip out to the car while I have a word with her. With a bit of luck she'll think you were there all the time.'

Danielle coloured. 'Why should you

pretend? Are you ashamed of being alone in your own house with the girl you're about to marry?'

He ran a hand through his hair. 'Please, Danny, don't be difficult, just do as I ask.'

She was silent as they drove back to The Royalty. John kept glancing at her, aware of her unease, sensing that it was more than just a natural frustration caused by the thwarting of their love-making. When the car drew to a halt outside the hotel he turned to look at her.

'I'm sorry, darling.'

She shook her head. 'It's not your fault,' she told him dully. Deep inside her there was a leaden feeling of anti-climax that had nothing to do with the untimely arrival of Mrs Downs.

He took her hand. 'Look, suppose we take some time off—spend a few days together somewhere—just the two of us. Away from here, where no one knows us?'

She turned to look at him, her eyes glittering angrily. 'Like a dirty weekend, you mean? No thanks. I wouldn't want you to do anything you might be ashamed of, John.' She got out of the car. 'Thanks for the lunch. Goodbye.' She ran into the building without a backward glance; passing a startled Sandra in the hall who stared in surprise at the owner of the hotel running up the stairs, her eyes bright with tears.

She ran a deep, hot bath and lay soaking in it, trying to wash off the disgust she felt for

52

herself. With all her heart she wished she had never set eyes on Adam Scott. He had brought her face-to-face with a side of herself she hadn't known existed. Twice in as many days she had made herself feel cheap and now she had hurt John too. And what was worse was the fact that she had *wanted* to hurt him—to punish him for not arousing in her the feelings she now knew herself capable of—for not being the lover she would always dream of—for not being Adam Scott! She clenched her fists tightly, trying to shut out the thought—feeling as though her whole world was standing on its head.

In her room she changed into a soft wool dress. Its vibrant green colour relaxed her a little as she sat before her dressing table mirror applying fresh make-up and combing her hair. Someone tapped gently on the door and she looked up.

'Who is it?'

'It's Sandra, Miss Denver.' The girl opened the door and looked anxiously in. 'I thought I'd better tell you that Mr Scott is back. He's been looking for you.'

Danielle laid down her comb wearily. 'Oh. Thank you, Sandra. I'll go down in a moment.'

The girl came into the room and closed the door, looking at her employer with concern. 'Are you all right, Miss Denver? Would you like me to get you anything? You're looking so tired.'

Danielle smiled at the girl. There wasn't a member of the staff whom she didn't know and like, but Sandra was a special favourite of hers. The girl had come to The Royalty on the Youth Opportunities Scheme two years before and had taken so well to the work that they had kept her on after her time was up. She had a special instinct for reception work, anticipating people's needs—knowing what they wanted almost before they did themselves and she was devoted to her young employer.

'I do feel tired,' Danielle confided. 'You've probably guessed that there are changes afoot. You'll learn all about them just as soon as I'm free to tell you.' She smiled reassuringly at the girl. 'Don't worry though. Your job is safe.'

'And you?' Sandra looked at her enquiringly. 'What will you be doing, Miss Denver? It wouldn't be the same here without you.'

'I wish others shared your feelings, Sandra,' Danielle sighed. 'But we shall just have to wait and see. Nothing is settled for the moment.'

'It must all be a great strain for you,' Sandra said sympathetically. 'No wonder you look tired. But at least you have Mr Peterson.'

Danielle stood up. The conversation was becoming decidedly awkward. 'I'd better come down now,' she said. 'Will you tell Mr Scott I'll see him in the lounge? And you'd better bring us some tea.' She made a mental note to remember to pour it this time.

He was waiting for her when she walked into the lounge and she saw with some dismay that they were the only two people in the room. He stood up as she crossed to him.

'It's good of you to spare me a few moments.'

She glanced at him out of the corner of her eye as she sat down in the chair next to him. Did his words hold a touch of sarcasm? But no, he looked pleasant enough as he nodded towards the tea tray on the table in front of them.

'Will you pour? I'm sure you must be ready for a cup of tea.'

Without replying she bent to busy herself with the teapot. He went on, explaining his last remark:

'I saw you come back a short while ago, with your fiance. Is everything all right?'

There was nothing she could do about the flush that crept into her cheeks as she handed him his cup. 'Of course. Why shouldn't it be?' Even to her own ears her voice sounded defensive.

He shrugged. 'No reason. It was just that you looked—well, tense.'

'Sandra said you wanted to see me,' she said, blatantly ignoring his observation.

'Yes.' He drained his cup and put it back on the table. 'I decided to telephone your uncle. I wanted to hear his reactions first-hand. Of course I had to wait until after lunch because of the time difference. He wouldn't have thanked me for getting him out of bed in the small hours.'

'Naturally.' She looked at him coolly, eyebrows arched. 'And did he approve of your idea?'

He nodded—rather smugly, she thought. 'I'm pleased to say he did. In fact he was delighted. He wants me to go ahead right away. I'd already made enquiries this morning and discovered that there are no other conference centres within easy reach. Also that there seems to be a more than adequate demand for one. My P.A. will be arriving tomorrow and I intend to get down to work at once. I've made an appointment with the planning people to thrash out any snags that may arise and I think I've found a good architect. He is coming to see me here at three o'clock tomorrow afternoon. I daresay you'd probably like to sit in on the meeting?'

Danielle felt slightly breathless at the speed with which he worked. 'Thank you. You don't let the grass grow under your feet, do you?'

He looked at her in surprise. 'I don't have time to.' He smiled suddenly disarmingly and the breath stopped in her throat. With the smile his face altered completely; the hardness of his mouth softening and the dark eyes lightening to a warm brown.

'I do have time for another cup of tea though. I hope you don't have to rush off. This seems a good time to relax and get to know one another a little better.'

'Is that necessary?' she asked, her heart quickening slightly. Getting to know each other, as he put it, was the last thing she wanted.

'Oh yes, I think it is,' he told her. 'I shall be needing your cooperation, Danielle. It will surely be easier if we are friends. Especially if you're still serious about becoming a Denver Group manager.'

'I'd have thought that after last night I'd be out of the running for *that*,' she said cuttingly.

He stiffened, his smile fading. 'That was uncalled for. I thought we shared the opinion that it was an unfortunate misunderstanding and agreed to wipe the slate clean. I've already apologised.'

When she didn't reply he leaned forward. 'Look, Danielle, it was all too obvious that you and your fiance had had a row when you came back this afternoon. And the fact that you aren't wearing your engagement ring confirms the fact. I hope it wasn't connected with me in any way.'

She started violently, staring at her left hand. She had taken off the ring when she had her bath. It was the first time since her engagement that she had forgotten to put it back on. Somehow it seemed symbolic. Her cheeks coloured as she sat looking unhappily down at her ringless hand. He hoped it wasn't in any way connected with him, did he? She wanted to shout at him: 'I was perfectly happy until *you* walked into my life. I thought I was in love with John—that my life was neatly laid out before me, a well-ordered plan. Who *else* do you think ruined it all for me?' Struggling to contain the seething rage inside her she said: 'Not at all. I took it off to wash and simply forgot to put it on again. As for us having a row, you're completely mistaken. We've been making plans for our house this afternoon. If everything here goes smoothly we shall be married as soon as possible. As for becoming a Denver Group manager, I've changed my mind. You were right; I *am* entering a new phase in my life.' She stood up, glad that the full skirt of her dress hid the trembling of her knees. 'Now, if you'll excuse me, there are things I must attend to.'

As she closed the door of the lounge behind her she paused to take a deep shuddering breath. She knew by his expression that she hadn't fooled Adam Scott for one moment. But more disturbingly, she hadn't fooled herself either. When she was near him all she could think of was his hard mouth on hers and the heady excitement of his caresses. She *couldn't* have fallen in love with the man in such a short time, surely? Things like that didn't happen in real life—*did* they?

58

CHAPTER FOUR

By five o'clock the following afternoon Danielle's head was spinning. Adam and Charles Townshend, the architect, had been discussing plans for the conference centre for two hours. The desk in front of them was strewn with papers and the wastepaper basket overflowed with discarded ideas. The plan they had finally settled on was laid out in rough in front of Adam. It was far more extensive than Danielle had imagined. In fact as far as she could see The Royalty would be almost unrecognisable when they were through with it. As well as conference facilities Adam planned to have a sports complex, with a swimming pool, sauna, and squash courts, built in the grounds so that businessmen and women attending could unwind and relax at the end of their day. Danielle's mind boggled at the figures being quoted for the cost. She wondered what her father would have thought of the idea.

As the two men brought their discussion to a close she stood up and went across to the telephone on her desk. 'I'll ring through to the kitchen for some tea, shall I? I'm sure we're all thirsty after all that talking.'

Charles looked at his watch. 'Well, I do have to go back to the office before I go home, but the tea does sound tempting.'

Sandra brought in the tray almost immediately, looking at Danielle as she placed it on the desk. 'There's a lady in Reception. She says she's booked in but I can't find anything in the book. Could you spare a minute?'

Danielle looked at Adam. 'Excuse me. I won't be a moment. Do help yourself to tea.'

In Reception a tall, striking brunette of about thirty stood tapping her foot impatiently. She turned when Danielle came up.

'Ah. I take it you are Miss Denver.'

Danielle nodded. 'That's right—and you are . . . ?'

'Roberta Hayward. You have a Mr Adam Scott staying here. He assured me he'd arranged accommodation but your receptionist doesn't seem to have me booked in.'

Danielle looked puzzled for a moment, then suddenly light dawned. 'Oh—are you his personal assistant?'

'Of course!' The other woman sounded indignant.

'We must have got our wires crossed,' Danielle explained. 'I entered the booking myself and I just put you down as Mr Scott's P.A. I was expecting you to be male and I told Sandra to look out for a gentleman. I'm sorry. You see, Adam referred to you as "Bobby".'

The cold look on Roberta Hayward's face melted slightly. 'Oh, I see. That's all right then. I'm sorry if I was sharp, but I've had rather a tiring flight and the thought of having to go out and find a room somewhere else was the last straw.'

Danielle took the key that Sandra handed her. 'I'll take you up myself,' she offered. 'Someone will bring up your luggage later.'

As she accompanied the other girl up to the second floor in the lift she couldn't help noticing that she looked every inch the efficient P.A. from her smoothly coiled dark hair and heavy-framed spectacles to the expensively tailored suit and high-heeled shoes.

'Have you come far?' she asked conversationally.

Roberta looked surprised. 'Didn't Adam tell you? I've been in America with Mr James. His own P.A. went sick the day before he flew out so I went instead. Adam wired me last night.' She frowned and shook her head. 'Or was it yesterday morning for you? I'm suffering from jet-lag I'm afraid.'

Danielle was impressed by her devotion to duty. 'And you came straight away!'

The other girl smiled. 'When Adam says *now* you can take it he means it! And Mr James's work was almost finished anyway.'

Danielle was learning more all the time about the high-powered Adam Scott. When he decided to make a move it seemed he swept all before him. 'He's certainly moving fast here,' she remarked. 'He's been in a meeting with the architect all afternoon. Between them they've made my head spin!'

The other girl laughed. 'That sounds like Adam all right.'

She was pleased with her room overlooking the lake and announced that she intended to get straight into the bath and then sleep off a little of her jet-lag.

'I know that the minute I see Adam he'll expect me to start working,' she said dryly.

'I'll have some tea sent up for you,' Danielle promised, noticing how weary the other girl looked. 'Dinner's from seven onwards. Perhaps I'll see you later.'

Downstairs again she was just in time to say goodbye to Charles Townshend, who was on the point of leaving. She went out onto the drive with Adam to wave him off. As the architect's car disappeared round the curve in the drive she turned to Adam.

'Your P.A. Miss Hayward, has arrived. There was a misunderstanding. I took it that "Bobby" was a man.'

He laughed. 'Poor Bobs. I'll slip up and fill her in about what's been happening. What's her room number?'

She touched his arm. 'I'd leave her for a while if I were you. She's suffering from jet-lag and badly in need of some rest. I told her

62

you'd see her at dinner.'

For a moment he looked as though he would disregard her advice, then he shrugged. 'Oh well, I suppose you're right.' He glanced at her. 'It's a beautiful afternoon. Shall we get some fresh air after being cooped up for hours? We could walk down and have a look at where the new buildings are to go.'

Her first instinct was to shy away from the idea. She had intended to ring John, but when she looked at her watch she realised that he would be probably somewhere between his office and home by now anyway. 'All right,' she said, falling into step beside him. It wouldn't do to let him think she was avoiding him.

'Well, you've been very quiet all afternoon. What did you think of the plan we worked out for the alterations?' he asked as they walked.

She shrugged. 'It's your baby. You can hardly expect it to excite me as much as it does you. This is the only home I've ever known. Soon it will be totally unrecognisable.'

He glanced at her. 'I can't say I've ever felt that strongly about mere bricks and mortar.'

'Nor, I suspect, about *mere* flesh and blood,' she countered. The moment she had said it she bit her lip. It had come out sounding so bitter. That was the last impression she had intended to convey.

He glanced at her speculatively. 'Mmm. I'm not your favourite person at the moment, am I, Danielle?'

She shrugged, trying to appear unconcerned. 'I haven't really thought about it.'

'Oh yes you have!' They had reached the low, sweeping branches of an ancient cedar tree and he suddenly grasped her arm and swung her round to face him. 'What's *really* bugging you?' he demanded, his dark eyes flashing dangerously. 'You need help and you're getting it from us—your uncle and me. You're hardly in a position to be arrogant about it. Ever since I arrived you've had this hostile attitude—apart from that first evening, that is,' he added in a tone that made her wince. He looked at her, eyes narrowing. 'If it weren't for the fact that we're related by marriage I'd . . .'

Her heart drummed uncomfortably as she faced him. 'Yes, go on—you'd what?' She shook off his arm furiously, her eyes blazing up at him. 'Really! I don't know how you have the nerve to stand there and speak to me like that. To come here, brashly walking all over everyone, including me. I believe you thought the place belonged to you the moment you walked in the door—the place and me with it! You're about the most insensitive person I've ever met!'

He threw up his hands in exasperation. '*God!* How many times do I have to apologise for an understandable mistake? If you really want to know, Danielle, it's *you* who should

64

apologise to me!'

'*Me?*' She spluttered incoherently, so angry she could hardly get the words out. 'What in heaven's n-name do *I* have to apologise for?'

'For deliberately misleading me, if you really want to know!' he shouted. 'What was I supposed to assume from that come-on act of yours? After all, when I kissed you you didn't exactly fight me off, did you?'

'Oh!' She took a step backwards, shaking her head. 'Oh—I think you're despic—*Oh!*' The rest of her sentence was lost as the heel of her shoe caught in one of the old tree's exposed roots. The next thing she knew she was sitting on the ground, staring up at him as he towered above her. The corners of his mouth twitched, then he gave a shout of laughter, his eyes dancing as he bent over her, holding out his hand.

'Here let me help you. You're not hurt, are you?'

She scrambled to her feet, her face scarlet. She was dangerously close to tears. It seemed she couldn't win with him. Everything she did went wrong. She couldn't even manage to look dignified! Adam turned her round and brushed the dust from her back a little more roughly than was necessary, she suspected. She turned to glare at him, her cheeks burning.

'Thank you, that's enough. I suppose that made your day?'

He turned her to face him, smiling down

into her eyes. 'Well, you have to admit, it eased the tension a little, didn't it?' She was acutely aware of the warmth of his hand through her sleeve as he asked, more seriously this time, the smile gone from his face as he saw her lip trembling. 'You *are* all right, aren't you—not hurt anywhere?'

Only my pride, she thought. It's only my confidence and peace of mind you've shattered with your arrogance. Composing her features, she said: 'I daresay I'll find a bruise or two later. Nothing serious.'

'Shall we call it quits then? Kiss and make up?' His face was very close to hers, his hands cupping her elbows as he drew her towards him.

She held her breath as she looked up at him. 'There's—no need . . .' His lips brushed hers softly and she began to panic as she felt the same sudden rise of excitement she had felt before. She tried to free herself but he held her fast, kissing her a second time, more thoroughly this time.

'Put your arms around me,' he commanded sharply as his lips left hers. 'Relax, damn it. It's nothing to get so tense about. It's no big deal—just a kiss.'

To her own surprise she did as he said, relaxing with a sigh, her head against his chest.

'That's better. You see? There's no need to make a Greek tragedy out of it. We could have quite a pleasant relationship if you weren't so

66

touchy and tense.' He stood for a moment, his chin resting on the top of her head and his arms wrapped firmly round her. Then he said kindly in a tone of voice she hadn't heard before: 'Believe me, I do understand how you feel, Danielle. I was uprooted from my home too, when my mother remarried. I know how it feels to be young and insecure—to resent an interloper, especially when ... well, we won't go into detail.' He looked down at her. 'The trick is to turn a disadvantage inside out and make it work for you. That's what I did.'

'Surely even you can see that I'm hardly in quite the same position,' she said quietly. 'I wouldn't know where to start.'

He held her a little away from him, smiling down into her eyes. 'I think this is as good a place to start as anywhere, don't you? I found out long ago that making enemies is a pretty negative occupation.'

Before she could reply his lips found hers again and once more she was lost in the heady thrill of his kiss till at last she found the strength to push him away, her cheeks pink and her eyes shining.

'You shouldn't behave like this. You know perfectly well that I'm engaged,' she told him breathlessly, appalled at the sensations that threatened to give her away at any minute.

He picked up her left hand and smiled wryly as he looked at the ring, now back in place.

'If you ask me, John Peterson is either a

very lucky, or a very *unlucky* man,' he said enigmatically.

'And just what does that mean?' she asked him.

He raised the hand to his face and held it against his cheek for a moment, his eyes glinting wickedly at her. 'Work it out, Danielle. Work it out.'

As they came in sight of the house again Danielle saw that John's car was parked in front of the entrance. Sandra called out to her as she came into Reception.

'Oh, there you are, Miss Denver. Mr Peterson is waiting for you in the office. I didn't know where you'd gone so I couldn't contact you.'

'It's all right, Sandra.' She looked at Adam. 'I'll see you at dinner.'

He nodded and made his way towards the staircase. Danielle took a deep breath and turned towards the office, feeling guilty. She owed John an apology. Better get it over with as quickly as she could.

He stood with his back towards her, at the window, turning as he heard her close the door. The expression in his eyes brought her up sharply. He looked guarded and suspicious, his eyes moving over her in a mistrustful way that surprised her. She began at once:

'John—I'm sorry about yesterday. I . . .'

'I should damn well think so too!' he snapped. 'I've been waiting for you to ring all

68

day.'

'We've been busy. The architect ...' she began. He didn't let her finish.

'You behaved extremely badly yesterday,' he told her. 'I don't know what came over you. I was quite prepared to forgive you this morning, but when the day went by and you hadn't rung ...'

She felt remorseful. Clearly he was far more hurt by her behaviour than she had expected. 'I know. I should have.' She went towards him, her hands held out placatingly. She was going to have to work hard to make up for what had happened yesterday. After all, it was her fault.

'Please, darling, don't be angry. All this upheaval has been a strain. I was going to ring you—honestly.' She took his hands and raised her face for his kiss but he pushed her away from him.

'Oh no! Don't think you can get round me like that again.' He shook his head at her. 'You've changed, Danielle. I don't know what's happened to you but you're suddenly different and I'm not sure that I like you this way.'

She stared at him. She didn't mind taking the blame but she wasn't going to be browbeaten. 'Then why are you here?' she asked him sharply.

He stood looking at her for a moment, his face a dull red. 'Because I think you owe me an apology.'

'I told you. I was going to ring you. You beat

me to it, that's all,' she told him indignantly. 'Anyway, I have already said I'm sorry.'

He clearly wasn't satisfied, angered by her defensive attitude. 'Now you listen to me, Danielle,' he said, his eyes glinting coldly behind the gold-rimmed spectacles as he wagged an admonishing finger in her face. 'You might think you've been running this place since your father died, but I can tell you now that you'd have been in a fine muddle if it hadn't been for me!'

She turned from him and went to the window, turning her back so that he wouldn't see the hurt in her eyes. 'I'm well aware of that, John,' she said quietly. 'And I have tried to show my gratitude. If I've failed . . .'

'I see. That's what it was, was it—*gratitude?*' He looked at her. 'Anyway, where have you been?' he demanded suddenly.

She turned to look at him. 'What do you mean, where have I been? I've been walking in the grounds. Adam and I went to look at the site of the new buildings he's planning.'

'*Walking*, eh?' He snorted. 'Your dress looks as though you've been *rolling* on the ground rather than walking over it!' He stepped up to her and grasped her arm painfully. 'Perhaps you were showing some of this *gratitude* of yours to Scott! I'm beginning to wonder if I know you at all, Danielle!' he said, his face close to hers. 'Yesterday afternoon was an eye-opener to me. Just how many men have there

70

been in your life?'

She stared at him, her eyes open wide. 'I don't understand. What are you saying, John?'

His lip curled. 'Don't play the innocent. If we're to be married I have a right to know. And you haven't explained this yet.' He picked up a piece of dried grass off the skirt of her dress and held it under her nose.

She took a step back from him. It was as though she were seeing him for the first time. This was a facet of John Peterson she had never met before and she didn't like it at all. 'You're mistaken, John,' she said unsteadily. 'I'm not your *property*. I don't have to explain my every movement to you. If you can't trust me—if your mind is so nasty; if you have such a low opinion of me then you deserve your own thoughts. But if you really want to know what happened, I caught my heel in a tree root and fell, though in your present mood I don't expect you to believe that!'

He looked at her for a moment, his eyes uncertain, then the door opened suddenly.

'I think I left my pen—Oh, I'm sorry.' Adam stood in the doorway, looking from one to the other.

'It's all right, John was just leaving,' Danielle said shakily.

They walked out to his car together in silence. As he unlocked the door John looked at her. 'I lost my temper, Danielle. I think you'll agree that I had good reason though.

71

Forgive me?'

She nodded. 'I should have got in touch with you this morning. I'm to blame.'

He took her hand. 'You've no idea what's been going through my mind all day. Can I take you to dinner this evening?'

She frowned. 'Adam's P.A. arrived an hour ago. I really feel I should be here to play hostess this evening. But you can come to dinner here if you like.'

He smiled wryly. 'Then I suppose I shall have to settle for that.'

As she watched his car disappear round the curve in the drive she heard the echo of his words in her head: 'You've changed, Danielle. I don't think I know you at all.'

He was right. She had changed. At the moment she felt she hardly knew herself. Adam Scott had upset her life completely. She felt guilty about John. He had every right to be cross with her. Yet his behaviour had angered her. He had acted as though she were one of his personal possessions. Was it a taste of what was to come after they were married?

'You're looking pensive. Not trouble, I hope?' Adam stood just inside the hotel's main entrance and it crossed her mind briefly that he had been watching John's departure. 'I hope you didn't mind my barging in like that,' he went on. 'I was passing the door and I heard raised voices. I thought a little timely intervention . . .'

She rounded on him: 'I don't know why everyone thinks I'm unable to handle my life without help!' she said tartly. 'John and I had a slight misunderstanding yesterday. He was here to put things right, that's all.'

'I see. I was right then. And are they—all right, I mean?'

Her eyes flashed with sudden exasperation. 'Oh—mind your own damn business!' she snapped then, turning abruptly, she went towards the stairs.

*　　*　　*

John arrived at seven and asked Sandra to ring through to her room. Danielle was still dressing and sent back a message that she would meet him in the bar in ten minutes. Perhaps she should have asked him to come up, but after his remarks that afternoon—and after Adam's misinterpretation of her actions on his first evening here she was beginning to think that everything she did was suspect.

She chose a dress of deep violet, a colour that set off the red-gold of her hair dramatically. Clasping her father's diamond around her neck she took a final look in the mirror. She had brushed out her hair loosely and it fell softly onto her shoulders; a little violet eye-shadow softened the defiant light in the green eyes. This evening she was determined to be her own woman. She had begun to feel like a leaf in the wind, tossed roughly this way and that by the men in her life. It was certainly time she took command of her own destiny. She sighed at her reflection in the mirror. 'If only I knew what that was,' she said aloud.

In the bar John had a dry Martini waiting for her. He was sitting at the bar, talking to Bill. When she came in he stood up and held out his hands, his eyes sweeping over her appreciatively.

'You look lovely—as always.' Tonight he was himself again, almost as though the ugly jealousy he had displayed that afternoon had never happened. Danielle tried hard to match his mood, but her heart wasn't in it.

'You're looking quite good yourself,' she told him with a smile, taking in the immaculate dark blue suit and striped tie. She sat up to the bar and sipped her drink.

'By the way, I don't think you need bother about playing hostess,' John remarked with some satisfaction. 'Scott and his P.A. seem to be pretty wrapped up in each other!' He nodded towards a table in the corner and Danielle glanced across to where Adam sat with Roberta Hayward. For a moment she hardly recognised the other girl. This evening she wore her dark hair loose, brushed smoothly to one side and caught up with a diamante clip to fall in a gleaming skein over one shoulder. The heavy horn-rimmed glasses were gone, revealing lustrous brown eyes and the clinging white dress she was wearing was clearly a designer model, bought perhaps during her recent stay in the States, Danielle speculated.

'An extremely attractive woman, isn't she?' John remarked. 'And it's quite clear that Scott needs no help at all in entertaining her!'

He was right. As Danielle watched, Adam leant forward to whisper something in the girl's ear, his dark head almost touching hers. She looked up at him, her eyes widening slightly as though his remark had been outrageous, then they laughed intimately together. Danielle was shocked to the core as a sudden pang of jealousy ripped through her. She coloured hotly as Adam looked up suddenly and caught her looking in their direction. He waved and she lifted her hand in response, then turned her attention to John.

'Shall we go in to dinner then?' she suggested brightly, getting to her feet. 'It looks as though it will be just the two of us. That's a relief, isn't it?'

It was almost as though Adam had deliberately chosen to sit where she could see them. All through the meal her eyes were drawn again and again towards the couple. They seemed so intimate, so happy in each other's company. John noticed it too, remarking halfway through the meal: 'I'd hazard a guess that she was a little more than

75

his P.A. wouldn't you?'

'I've no idea,' she said stiffly. 'It's really nothing to do with us, is it?'

John's eyes watched them as they rose from their table and walked towards the door, Adam's hand resting lightly and easily on Roberta's waist.

'You're staring at them,' Danielle hissed irritatedly. She hated the look of smugness on John's face and the thoughts that were all too clearly passing through his mind; chiefly because they echoed her own. She touched his arm. 'Shall we have coffee in the lounge?'

He turned to look at her in surprise. 'Can't we go up to your flat?'

She sighed. 'Not this evening if you don't mind, John, I'm tired.'

He looked at her anxiously. 'You're not still worried about the things I said this afternoon, are you? Surely you know I didn't mean them?' He looked at her, trying to assess the reason for her silence. 'I think waiting is making us both edgy,' he went on. 'I feel we should get married as soon as possible—even before things are settled here. I think you might get things into perspective better if you were away from the place.'

'That's ridiculous,' she said tersely. 'How can I possibly arrange a wedding with all there is to think about at present?' Discussing wedding plans was the last thing she wanted to do this evening. Besides, it annoyed her that she should be expected to forget so easily his proprietorial attitude this afternoon.

'It could be a quiet affair,' he suggested.

She shook her head firmly. 'No, John. Please let me end one chapter of my life properly before I begin another.'

She walked with him to his car. In the darkness he took her in his arms and kissed her ardently. Releasing her a moment later, he looked down wryly into her eyes.

'Oh dear. You *are* tired, aren't you?'

'I'm sorry, John,' she muttered unhappily. 'It's been quite a day.'

Up in her room she undressed and slipped into her dressing gown. As she took off her make-up she found herself wondering what Adam and Roberta were doing and pulled a face at herself in the mirror, despising herself for the direction her thoughts were taking. To Adam Scott a kiss meant nothing, he had implied as much this afternoon. It was simply a pleasant way of communicating. She sighed. She obviously had a lot to learn about life— about men and sex. She had tried to prove to herself that what she felt for John was really love and the result had been worrying and disruptive. Not only was she unsure of herself; John no longer trusted her either.

Maybe he had good reason. Maybe she wasn't ready to marry anyone yet!

CHAPTER FIVE

When Danielle walked into her office the following morning at nine o'clock she hardly recognised it. All the furniture had been rearranged to accommodate a mass of electronic office equipment. Bobby Hayward was seated at the desk Danielle had had brought in and was busy working on a word processor which seemed to Danielle's unpractised eye a mass of keys bearing strange words. The other girl looked up as she entered. This morning she was once more a picture of efficiency, wearing a neat navy dress, the dark hair neatly coiled and the spectacles in evidence again.

'Good morning,' she said briskly. 'I hope you don't mind? There was so much to do, I thought I'd better get on with it.'

Danielle looked round at the equipment that made the office look like something out of a science-fiction movie.

'When did all this arrive?' she asked.

'Oh, apparently Adam got onto a local office equipment firm yesterday afternoon, just before they closed,' Bobby explained. 'They were very good. They had it all here and set up at half-past eight.'

'I'm impressed,' Danielle remarked dryly.

'Oh, that's Adam,' Bobby laughed. 'He

seems to have the knack of getting people to do what he wants. I expect he casually let slip a hint that there could be a good contract in it if they played ball. When this place is reorganised we shall be needing quite a lot of electronic equipment.'

Danielle bent closer to peer at the monitor. 'It's fascinating. How does it work?'

The other girl explained the code words on the key-pad and gave her a short demonstration. 'Once you've worked with one of these you wouldn't want to go back to the old method,' she said. 'It almost cuts out the need for a secretary, though I would be grateful if I could borrow yours to make a few phonecalls for me this afternoon. There are certain people I can't get hold of and Adam and I plan to be out after lunch for the rest of the day.'

'Yes, of course,' Danielle said abstractedly, watching as the other girl printed out in seconds a lengthy letter which would have taken her half an hour on the typewriter.

'It's amazing, I'd love to try it myself,' she said.

'Help yourself, I've almost finished,' Bobby invited. 'You know, you're quite a surprise.' She looked at Danielle, her head on one side. 'I don't know why but I got the impression that you were younger. I had this image of a little girl with pigtails somehow. I wasn't prepared for an attractive, grown young woman.'

Danielle smiled. 'Thank you.'

'Has Adam made a pass at you yet?'

Danielle looked up, blushing at the other girl's sudden and unexpected question. By her casual tone it was nothing unusual for Adam to make passes at female associates. She worked closely with him and would know his general attitude and behaviour towards the opposite sex.

Bobby took her hesitation and her sudden colouring for confirmation. 'Ah—I see that he has. Don't let it throw you. Adam's used to getting anything he wants and when I saw you . . .' Bobby left the remark unfinished. 'He just ploughs in—doesn't take no for an answer. I suppose that's the secret of his success— being positive. If you gave him the brush-off it would take some swallowing on his part, but he'll respect you for it.' She deftly went through the process of storing the letters she had written on disk, then switched the machine off. 'I'm always telling him that there's a difference between a business deal and a personal relationship. He never seems to learn though.' She looked at Danielle. 'I must say he's got a nerve—you being engaged. Oh, by the way, he asked me to pass on a message to you. He would like to speak to all the staff at eleven o'clock if that's convenient.'

'Oh—I'd better arrange it now then,' Danielle said. 'You can tell him I'll ask them to assemble in the staff sitting room.'

'And there's something else. I telephoned your uncle. He's on his way over. He'll want to stay for a couple of days and take a good look round, so if you could have a room prepared for him . . .'

Danielle gasped. 'You certainly work fast!' She frowned. 'But surely it's the middle of the night over there at the moment?'

'Oh, I rang him last night after dinner,' Bobby explained. 'Adam and I put in a couple of hours' work after we'd eaten.'

Danielle nodded. 'Of course.' She felt slightly dizzy. It was all so high-powered! She went off to pass on the message to the staff, her thoughts still preoccupied by Bobby's remarks. Had he seen her simply as another challenge—another goal to be won and chalked up to bolster his ego? Was he really so cold-blooded that he didn't care whose feelings he trampled on just so long as he got what he wanted?

At five to eleven the staff were gathered. There was a buzz of anticipation in the air. For weeks now they had been unsettled and apprehensive. Rumours had been rife since Matthew Denver's death. Were they to lose their jobs? What changes would the new management bring about? Would Danielle Denver be staying on? It seemed that this morning all would be revealed and the atmosphere in the staff sitting room was tense and electric.

81

At precisely eleven Adam arrived and took his place at the table Danielle had placed at one end of the room for him. An expectant silence fell as he looked round at them. Very carefully, he explained his plan and reassured them that all those who wished to stay would be found jobs. For most the work would be almost unchanged but he finished by urging them to think over carefully what he had told them, asking the kitchen staff to remain so that he could explain the changes he proposed to make and their part in them.

Danielle glanced at Arthur to see how he was taking it, but his lean, craggy face and shrewd blue eyes gave nothing away, even after Adam had asked him to stay on after the others had left and had spoken to him at some length about the new equipment he planned to install and the streamlined regimen he intended to put into practice, the chef's face remained enigmatic.

As Arthur left Danielle made to follow him but Adam caught her eye and beckoned her over.

'Can I have a word, Danielle?'

She crossed the room to where he stood. 'Yes?'

'I expect Bobby has told you that your uncle is due tomorrow?'

'She did mention it.'

'I really need him to okay the plans before I ask Charles Townshend to go ahead, you see.'

'Of course.'

A flicker of irritation crossed his brow at her taciturn response. 'I didn't want you to think I was arranging things over your head' he explained.

'Very good of you' she muttered. Her heart was thudding unevenly in her chest as he stood close to her. She told herself it was because of what she had learned from Bobby—that anger made her hate to be near him, but deep inside she knew that any second she was going to have to admit to herself that it was more. 'If that's all then . . .' She made to move away but he caught her arm.

'You're looking a bit peaky this morning. Look, Bobby and I are going out this afternoon. She doesn't know this part of the country and I promised to show her round. The poor girl has been working hard almost since the moment she arrived. Why don't you come with us?'

She shook her head. 'I wouldn't dream of butting in,' she said stiffly.

He laughed. 'Don't be silly. Of course you wouldn't be butting in. We could have tea somewhere. Bobby has a fancy for one of those old-fashioned tea shop places. It'll be fun. I haven't relaxed since I arrived here.'

'I'm afraid I'm not in the mood,' she told him. Even to her own ears she sounded stuffy. 'I have a million things to do anyway,' she said quickly.

She watched them leave from the office window soon after lunch, her eyes wistful. Bobby Hayward looked informally attractive in a pale blue linen skirt and a tightly fitting tee-shirt that left little to the imagination. She was laughing as she climbed into the sleek Mercedes beside Adam, who looked truly relaxed in close-fitting jeans and an open-necked shirt. As the car moved silently away down the drive Maggie looked at her speculatively.

'There isn't anything much to do this afternoon. Why don't you take some time off too?'

Danielle shrugged restlessly. 'What would I do?'

The older woman smiled. 'I could think of a dozen things. See a film, have your hair done—a facial, or even the sheer luxury of a quiet afternoon with a tray of tea and a book!'

Danielle pulled a face. She was getting tired of being told how pale and wan she was looking. 'Are you trying to tell me something, Maggie? Do I look in need of some of those things?'

Maggie pursed her lips. 'Well—since you ask, you *are* looking a little tired. Come on, what's it to be? Shall I telephone and make an appointment for you?'

Danielle gave it a moment's thought and then made up her mind. 'Oh—all right. I'll go into Cirencester and have the full works. It'll make me *feel* better if nothing else!'

It was half-past five when Danielle came out of the beauty salon. After a manicure, facial and hair-do she felt refreshed and her reflection in the mirror told her it had been well worth it. Looking at her watch she realised she had taken more time than she intended and she drove back to Kingswood hurriedly. Deep inside she had an odd, uneasy feeling that all was not well. A sixth sense told her that she was needed back at The Royalty and her stomach churned with apprehension as she drove, impatient with the slowness of the rush-hour traffic. She tried to talk herself out of the feeling. After all, what could have gone wrong in such a short time? she reasoned, but the feeling persisted.

She put her car away in the garage and went in by the staff entrance at the back. In the corridor Sandra met her, her face tense and anxious.

'Oh, Miss Denver, thank goodness you're here. I've just telephoned the beauty salon but they'd closed for the day. Something awful's happened.'

Danielle's heart gave a lurch. So she hadn't been wrong after all. 'What is it?' she asked.

'It's Arthur.'

'Arthur? What is it—tell me? Is he ill?'

'He's gone!'

Danielle stared at the girl. '*Gone?* What do you mean, gone?'

'Mr Scott sacked him, Miss Denver—sent him packing. He was terribly angry.'

'But *why*?' A feeling of cold panic gripped her heart.

'It was awful. He was drunk—Arthur, I mean. I'm afraid it looked as though he'd been drinking all afternoon. Mr Scott came back about half an hour ago and went into the kitchen. He found him trying to start dinner and he just—just told him to get out.'

'Oh my God!' Danielle wailed. 'Poor Arthur. I wonder where he went? Anything could have happened to him! I must go and look for him.'

'*Oh no you won't!* You'll get your things off and come and help me! We've got an emergency on our hands!'

Danielle spun round to see Adam standing in the kitchen doorway, a large white apron tied round his waist and his shirt sleeves rolled up to the elbows. His eyes glittered, dark as coal as he glared at her.

'This is what comes of being over-familiar with staff. Come on, there's a lot to do. I've looked at the book and there are thirty guests and four non-resident couples booked for dinner—and just over an hour to have everything ready!'

In the kitchen the other members of the staff stood around stunned and white-faced. Adam was an awesome sight, fury emanating from him as he towered over them, an evil-looking kitchen knife in his hand. He waved it towards a small table covered with ingredients.

'I suggest you help by making the sauces. I understand that you don't have a sauce chef.'

Danielle stared coldly at him and then at her cowering staff. How dared he treat them like this—and to *sack Arthur*! It was unbelievable! 'If there's an emergency it's of your own making. Arthur must be found. You obviously over-reacted. He never let a few drinks stop him from carrying out his duties as everyone here knows and could have told you if you'd taken the trouble to ask!'

Adam's eyes widened as he stared at her. 'Are you telling me that this is a regular habit of his? And you kept it to *yourself* !'

'No it isn't!' she protested. 'Arthur hasn't had a drink for ages. You must have really upset him to make him start again.'

'I did nothing of the sort. All I did was to tell him about the changes I had in mind.' Adam brandished the knife in exasperation. 'Good God! I'd have thought it would have *pleased* him to know that from now on things were about to be made easier! Just look at this lot!' He swept an arm round the kitchen. 'You'd think we were living in the Middle Ages. Hasn't anyone here ever heard of microwaves?' He glared at the staff, who stood about numbly. 'What the hell are you all doing, standing there like dummies? Get on with it, can't you?'

Galvanised into action they scuttled away to their various tasks. Danielle turned angrily and made to flounce out of the kitchen. If he wanted to pursue the argument he could follow her. She wasn't going to stand and spar with him in front of the staff. But a moment later she was shocked to find herself grasped by the arm and hauled back.

'I think you're forgetting something!' An angry pair of eyes burned into hers as Adam thrust an apron into her hands. 'If I'm prepared to put myself out the least you can do is help,' he hissed quietly. 'Now—you don't want to make *another* scene in front of your employees, do you? So get your coat off and get to work. If you do as I say we might just make it.'

She gaped at him, momentarily lost for words. 'But—but Arthur! Anything could have happened to him!' she protested.

'If, as you say, Arthur can put on dinner for fifty in that state he's not likely to come to much harm, is he? You can get up a search party for him later if you want to—but not until we've got this meal prepared!'

Forced to see his point, she had little choice. During the hour that followed she worked hard and in spite of the bitter resentment she felt for Adam Scott she couldn't help grudgingly admitting the efficient way he stepped into Arthur's shoes. The rest of the staff recognised his obvious command too, following the orders he barked out, quickly and silently and by seven everything on the menu was cooked to a perfection that even Arthur could not have faulted. Danielle, who had never cooked on this scale in her life, was astonished at the array of sauces she had created, all with the help of Adam's expert, step-by-step directions. Quite clearly his thorough early training had paid off. Once the serving had begun he stripped off his apron and looked at her.

'Well, that's that. I'm going to have a bath. Shall we eat together later?'

'No thank you!' She pulled off her own apron. 'I shan't be able to eat a thing until I've found out what's happened to Arthur. There's more to employing people than shouting orders at them, you know. At least there always has been at The Royalty!'

In her room she rang down to Reception. To her relief Sandra told her Arthur had rung and left a number where he could be contacted. She dialled it eagerly. It appeared that the chef was staying with a friend who assured Danielle that he was safe and sobering up fast. When he came to the telephone, Arthur was contrite.

'I've let you down, Danny. I'm sorry. I wouldn't have had it happen for the world.'

'Don't worry, Arthur. Just as long as you're all right,' she assured him. 'When will you be back?'

There was a pause. 'I think we must face the fact that the new boss won't want me back,' Arthur said bleakly. 'Anyway, I don't really fancy ending my days doing the sort of mass production he's planning. I've always had a secret plan, you know—it's been a sort of pipe-dream of mine for years. I've been thinking—if I don't do it now it'll be too late, so maybe this has given me just the push I needed.'

'What dream, Arthur? What are you talking about?' she urged, wondering if he was still a little drunk. 'You're not just saying this, are you?'

'No, Danny, I'm not. Give me a few days and I'll be in touch with you again. And don't worry about me, there's a good girl.'

She replaced the receiver with a sigh. Adam Scott was ruthless and uncompromising. He obviously didn't give a damn whose life he wrecked as long as he considered the end result was worth it. She wanted to tell him so—*now*, while she was still angry.

She strode purposefully along the corridor and knocked sharply on his door. He opened it wearing a bathrobe, a towel in his hand and his hair still wet and ruffled from the bath.

'Oh, it's you.' He held the door open for her. 'You'd better come in.'

She stepped into the room and came straight to the point. 'You might be interested to know that I've located Arthur and he's all right,' she told him, her voice quavering.

'I never doubted that he would be,' he told her casually, rubbing at his wet hair. 'A man who can get away with what he obviously has for all these years quite clearly has a well-developed sense of self-preservation!'

Fury boiled up inside her. 'Arthur was a good friend of my father's. He was like another member of the family to me. More like an uncle than your stepfather ever was! He never *ever* let us down and he never would have.' She stared coldly at him, wishing her heart would slow down. It was hammering so fast she felt almost faint. 'You—you can't treat everyone like a machine, you know. People are flesh and blood—with *feelings!*'

He looked at her, his brows gathering in a frown. 'Look—when I found him reeling about in the kitchen this afternoon it was clear that someone had to make a decision,' he told her. 'You weren't here so I had to make it myself. I'm still convinced that I did the right thing.' He threw the towel down angrily. 'And I'm also convinced that you owe me a little gratitude instead of coming in here shrieking like an outraged vixen!' He glared down at her. 'If it hadn't been for me you would have had a lot of very dissatisfied clients on your hands this evening.'

She stood her ground, meeting his gaze with blazing eyes. 'On the contrary, if it hadn't been for *you* Arthur would have cooked the meal as usual!' she countered, lifting her chin defiantly.

He shook his head at her, his lip curling cynically. 'And you asked me if you could stay on as a Denver Group manager! I can tell you now, Danielle—there is *no way* you'd ever get a job with us. We run *hotels*, not charitable institutions!'

She took a step towards him, her heart hammering so hard now that she could scarcely breathe and her voice came out in a series of gasps. 'I—wouldn't work for you— Adam Scott if—if I hadn't a penny in the world! I'd—I'd rather *beg in the gutter* than ask you for anything. But I do have something I'd like to give you—and it's *this*!' She raised her hand and slapped him hard across the cheek.

The next moment she found herself reeling with shock as she received a stinging slap in return. Her hand flew to her smarting face as she stared up at him and instantly his hands shot out to steady her.

'Danielle! I'm sorry—it was a reflex action. I shouldn't . . .'

She struggled, tears welling-up in her eyes. She had gone too far and she knew it. Never before in her life had she lost control like that. And he—Adam Scott, had made her do it. She would never forgive him for that. 'Let me go!' she insisted. Was he going to make her stay so that he could watch her humiliation? The tears were trickling helplessly down her cheeks now. She swallowed hard, lowering her eyes. 'I—

hate you for making this happen,' she muttered. 'Really hate you!'

'No you don't. You're just overwrought,' he said soothingly. 'Here, calm down. I'll get you a brandy in a minute.' He held her fast, one hand pressing her head into his shoulder. His arms imprisoned her, making it clear that he wasn't going to let her go and suddenly she was acutely aware of the fact that he was obviously naked under the robe. It was open to the waist and as he pressed her close her face almost touched the thick, dark hair that curled on his chest. Her senses tingled at the clean male scent of him and the warmth and hardness of his strong body. In a strange way they seemed to calm her and inflame her senses at one and the same time. Slowly she felt the anger drain from her, leaving her weak and exhausted.

He raised her face, one finger under her chin, looking down at her. His eyes, calm now, carried an expression she couldn't read—deep and warm. 'Have dinner with me, Danielle? You'll feel better when you've eaten.'

She shook her head. 'I can't face people tonight.'

'We'll have it brought up here. I really think we should talk.'

'What could there possibly be to talk about?' she asked breathlessly.

'I think we might find something we have in common,' he said, laughing softly. 'If we could

93

stop rowing for long enough to discover it.' His lips brushed hers and she stood still within the circle of his arms as though mesmerised, unable to move. His arms tightened round her, one hand moving down her spine to press her thighs against his. 'You're not afraid to be alone with me, are you, Danielle?' His voice was low and husky as his lips took hers, moving sensuously and demandingly, coaxing her own into a response.

Gathering every ounce of self-control she pushed him away. 'No—Don't! That's your way, isn't it? You think you can conquer me like that just because I'm a woman. Well you can't because—because I won't let you!'

Bursting out into the corridor she almost collided with a startled Bobby Hayward, who stood staring after her curiously. Back in her room she slammed the door and leaned against it, closing her eyes and trying to still the painful throbbing in her chest and throat. Why did he have such power over her when she disliked everything he stood for? The worst of it was that he was obviously aware of the effect he had on her. It was so humiliating! She sank onto the bed, burying her face in the pillow in an attempt to blot out the image of them—Adam and Bobby, laughing at her right at this minute in his room. He would no doubt be recounting the way he had ordered her about in front of her own kitchen staff that evening and then calmed her anger so easily with his blatant sexuality. How could she ever hold up her head in the house again?

*   *   *

James Denver's flight was due at three-thirty the following afternoon and Adam had sent Roberta Hayward in a hired car to the airport to meet him. Danielle had the best room in the hotel prepared for him. After yesterday she didn't want any more hang-ups.

First thing that morning she had telephoned the agency. Luckily they had a good chef available who was prepared to work on a trial basis with a view to being taken on by the Denver Group if he proved satisfactory.

Since her disastrous attempt at putting Adam in his place last night she had kept out of his way, but as the time for James Denver's arrival drew near she found herself becoming increasingly nervous. During the long hours of a wakeful night she had tried to plan her future. Clearly she couldn't work with Adam, so it seemed inevitable that she must say goodbye to The Royalty once and for all. She wondered how much money she would get if she asked her uncle to buy her out. She didn't like the thought of being totally dependent on John once they were married. Maybe she could start a small business of her own. But first she must talk to her uncle—preferably alone.

She saw her opportunity later that evening. The four of them had dinner together, Adam and Bobby, Danielle and her Uncle James. He was very different from what she had imagined. Somehow she thought he would resemble her father, but he did not. A few years younger than Matthew Denver, he was every inch the successful businessman from his hand-made shoes to his silver hair and neatly trimmed beard. During dinner he was charming and attentive to her, but all the time he watched her with shrewd light blue eyes. They talked informally during the meal, but over the sweet course she could see that he was anxious to be done with small-talk. Obviously he would want to have a long talk with Adam. If she wanted to see him tonight she must stake her claim.

'I'd like to speak to you alone, if you can spare me a few minutes, Uncle James,' she ventured.

He patted her hand. 'My time is all yours, Danielle. When shall it be?'

'If we could have coffee in my office, perhaps . . . ?' She smiled at him.

'Of course. No time like the present.' He turned to the others with a benign smile. 'I'll see you two later.'

In the office she poured him a coffee and came straight to the point: 'I wanted to ask you a favour, Uncle.'

He sipped his coffee, looking at her over the

rim of the cup with a smile that masked his appraisal of her. 'Ask away, my dear.'

Encouraged, she went on: 'I thought at first there might be a future for me here, but I now see that there won't be. I'm engaged to be married and as you know, money is in rather short supply at the moment, so I wondered if—if you would buy me out?'

He frowned, putting his cup down slowly on the table. 'Buy you out? I'm afraid I don't understand.'

She moistened her dry lips. It wasn't going to be as easy as she had first thought. 'Well, I know Daddy didn't leave a will but as his only child I'm surely entitled to a share of his estate?'

He shook his head. 'I don't think you quite understand, my dear. Matthew was in a great deal of debt.'

'I realise that. But there was enough money to pay most of it off—wasn't there?'

He nodded. 'Officially, yes. What you don't know—can't be expected to know, I suppose, is that Matthew owed *me* a lot of money.'

Danielle's mouth dropped open in surprise. 'You? But I thought you'd had nothing to do with each other for years.'

He sighed. 'Obviously he kept it from you. It was sad. After your mother died he was desolate. He started gambling and it became an incurable habit. He borrowed from me when his creditors threatened to take him to court. This place was mortgaged to the hilt. It was that or losing The Royalty.'

Slowly the truth sank in. 'So—there's no money?' she said. 'In effect The Royalty is already yours?'

'I'm afraid so. I have papers to prove it,' he told her. 'And even so there are still several thousand pounds outstanding.'

'You mean—I not only have no home but I'm in your debt as well?' She stared at him in dismay.

He shook his head. 'No, no, my dear. Blood is thicker than water after all. I'm quite prepared to forget the debt.'

Her chin went up. 'No! I owe it to Daddy to pay it off somehow or other.'

He looked at her shrewdly. 'You said money was in short supply. May I ask how you propose to settle a debt like that? What will this fiance of yours think of it? He may not fancy taking on a wife with a large debt round her neck.'

'I don't care,' she told him defiantly. 'I'll find some way. I *must*.'

'Mmm. You're like your mother, Danielle, both in looks and spirit. I can just picture her saying the same thing.' He was silent for a moment or two, then he said suddenly: 'I have a proposition to put to you. I warn you—at first you may not like the idea, but all I ask is that you sleep on it. You can tell me tomorrow what your answer is.'

She looked at him hopefully. 'All right. What is it?'

He helped himself to more coffee, taking his time before speaking, weighing his words carefully. 'Tell me, what do you think of Adam?'

She looked at him in surprise, a feeling of unease beginning in the pit of her stomach as she answered guardedly: 'I—he's clearly very good at his job.'

He smiled. 'That's not *quite* what I meant. Do you like him—get along with him?'

She frowned. 'Well enough,' she said evasively. 'Why?'

'I've got a job for him,' he told her. 'I want him to go to Switzerland within the next day or two; to look at a property I hope to buy. How would you feel about going with him?'

She shook her head. 'Me? I don't understand. Why should *I* go?'

'I'll be quite direct with you, my dear, though of course, what I have to say is in strict confidence. He's getting rather too close to Bobby Hayward for my liking.' He looked at her with narrowed eyes, trying to assess her reaction. 'I don't want to see him get hooked by her. That young woman has an eye to the main chance. She's set her sights on a directorship if I'm not very much mistaken and as Adam's wife she'd be entitled to it. I know you've been trained as a secretary. I'd like you to go with him. I'll find a vital job for Bobby here.'

'But for what purpose?' Danielle asked, hoping against hope that his plan wasn't the one lurking darkly at the back of her mind.

He paused: 'I want you to take his mind off her, my dear. I'm sure you know how to do that.' The hard blue eyes smiled suggestively into hers. 'Well, there it is. Adam appreciates a pretty girl and I can see that he's already attracted to you so it shouldn't be difficult—or too unpleasant. He's quite a presentable young man and Switzerland is a beautiful, romantic place.'

She fumed at his calm attitude to what she considered a cheap deception. It seemed her uncle was another businessman accustomed to using people for his own ends, even members of his own family! 'Perhaps you've forgotten, Uncle, I'm engaged!' she reminded him tartly.

He shrugged, unmoved. 'I see no reason why that should make any difference. You simply remove your ring and allow Adam to think it's off. Your fiance need never know because by the time you get back the affair will be over.'

Anger rose in her chest, almost choking her. 'I—I've never heard of anything so devious and deceitful in my life!' she exploded.

He chuckled. 'Thank you. I thought it was rather good myself!'

She stood up. 'And of course I don't need time to think about it. The answer is no!'

His smile dissolved, revealing the cold steel underneath. 'Ah—but you see, I do have a trump card,' he told her icily. 'I was hoping I wouldn't have to play it but I can see that you have scruples and they, I'm afraid, are a luxury you can't afford. The alternative is this: Either you do this little thing for me and we wipe the slate clean, or I give you back The Royalty—*complete with all its debts!*'

CHAPTER SIX

Danielle felt stunned as she stared into the ice-blue eyes of the man who was her father's brother. Surely all this must be a bad dream. The minutes ticked by as she struggled to take in all he had just told her. At last she found her voice.

'It seems I have no choice but to do as you say,' she said reluctantly. 'But I still don't understand. If all you have told me is true, surely it would have come out after Daddy died.' Her voice was weak with shock. 'John, my fiance, would have known about it. He's our accountant and he went through all Daddy's records—the books and everything.'

James Denver shook his head. 'All my loans to your father were kept on a strictly personal basis. Nothing went through the business. You need have no fears, Danielle; no one need ever know of your father's weakness. It's between you and me now.'

'Just so long as I do as you say, you mean?' She glanced at him warily and his silence confirmed her dread. Slowly the devious, convoluted nature of her uncle's mind was unfolding itself to her.

'You deliberately kept it all on a strictly personal basis because it suited you, not out of kindness,' she said, thinking aloud. 'It was more convenient to let The Royalty remain in Daddy's name, even though it was virtually yours. You knew we'd have no choice but to turn to you when he was finally forced to give up the struggle.' She looked at him, her eyes demanding the truth. 'I suppose Adam knew all about it?'

'No. Adam knew—*knows* nothing. He's an employee as far as business goes and as such he follows my orders like the rest.'

'And now *I'm* an employee too and obliged to follow orders! That's what you're really saying, isn't it?' she said bitterly.

'I'm glad you're facing up to it, my dear. Much better in the end.'

'Suppose I refuse?' she challenged. 'I could see the bank manager—get a loan to begin again. I have lots of ideas. I'm sure he'd help me.'

James Denver stroked his beard thoughtfully. 'Try if you wish by all means, my dear. But I think you'll find that your youth and inexperience—not to mention the deplorable state of the books and the amount of money owing . . .' He wasn't quite able to keep the triumph out of his voice as he saw her shoulders slump. Reaching forward, he touched her hand. 'Danielle—see sense, my dear. What I'm asking isn't so terrible, surely? When you return from Switzerland you can begin again with a clean slate. Start life anew.'

She frowned, withdrawing her hand from his. Did he honestly imagine it was as easy as that? Did he think everyone was as cold and impersonal as he was himself? 'You said you wanted Adam's mind taken off Bobby,' she said. 'yet if they're as close as you say, surely he'll start seeing her again when he gets back from Switzerland. After all, they'll be working together again.'

'No, they won't!' James Denver's voice was as hard as steel as he clipped the words out. 'But that is my problem and needn't concern you. All you have to do is relax and enjoy Switzerland—and exercise your considerable charm on Adam, of course.' He smiled. 'I'm sure most young women would consider it a small price to pay for such a reward.' He stroked the beard again. 'A cushy option, one might almost say!'

She felt trapped. Feverishly she cast about in her mind for a way out.

'What about The Royalty?' she asked. 'It won't run itself while I'm away. And what am I supposed to tell my fiance?'

'As for the hotel, I think you can safely leave it in my hands,' he told her calmly. 'I do have a *little* experience in running one! As for your fiance—and anyone else who needs to know where you are, I suggest you say that you have to go abroad to clear up the last of your father's affairs.' He seemed pleased with the irony of his words. 'After all, it's true in a way, isn't it? Perhaps it would be better if you thought of it that way yourself. It might help you to overcome your aversion to the idea.'

Defeated, she got to her feet. 'When do you want me to leave?' she asked wearily.

'The sooner the better. Can you be ready the day after tomorrow?'

She gasped. 'So soon? Do I have to travel with Adam?'

He shook his head. 'No. I don't want you to mention it to him. Simply leave. I want you to be at the hotel when he arrives.' He smiled benignly. 'I want it to be a little surprise for him. You see—I'm really just an old romantic at heart!'

Danielle was tempted to tell him the word she would have used to describe him but she bit the remark back. 'So I'm not to tell anyone where I'm going?' she concluded.

'That's right. All you have to do is pack your prettiest clothes, a pencil and shorthand pad and get on the plane.' He took a wallet from an inside pocket and extracted an envelope

104

which he handed to her. 'Here is your air ticket. I take it your passport is in order?'

She stared at him. 'You went ahead and booked even before you'd spoken to me! You knew I'd have no choice but to accept your proposal?'

'I knew you'd see sense. Let's put it that way,' he told her soothingly.

*   *   *

Two days later Danielle sat in the departure lounge at Heathrow, waiting for the nine-thirty flight to Zurich to be called. She still felt slightly dazed as she sipped her coffee and watched the endless panorama of people.

The last thirty-six hours had been hectic and worrying with packing to do and arrangements to make. Not the least of her worries had been the story she had had to concoct to explain her absence—especially when it came to John.

When she had telephoned him at his office yesterday morning and told him she would have to be away for the next few days he had asked interminable questions. It had taken all of her wit and inventiveness to satisfy his curiosity as to the reason for her sudden departure. She squirmed even now as she remembered the deception she was practising, even though she had told him no actual lies. Deception had never come easily to her, though lately it seemed she was being forced into practising it more and more! As she drank her coffee she went over the telephone conversation again in her mind.

'John—I have to be away for a few days. I have to go to Switzerland for my uncle—on an errand.'

'I don't understand, Danielle. What errand? And why do *you* have to go?'

She had been glad to be at the other end of a telephone line so that he couldn't see her face as she replied: 'There isn't anyone else he can send.' Her mouth felt dry. 'I don't know very much about it myself yet, but I'm rather dependent on him at the moment, so I can hardly refuse.'

'Would you like me to come with you?' John had offered. 'I'm pretty busy at the moment but I think I could wangle a couple of days.'

Her heart quickened with alarm. Surely he wasn't going to make life even more difficult for her by insisting on coming too? 'No! It's better if I go alone,' she told him quickly. 'It may take longer than a couple of days anyway.'

'Well, if you're sure.' She was grateful for the unmistakable relief in his voice. 'It would be rather difficult for me to get away just now. Whereabouts in Switzerland, by the way?'

'I'm flying to Zurich tomorrow,' she told him evasively.

'Well, at least let me drive you to the airport.'

'No! I have to catch the nine-thirty flight,

106

which means I'll have to make a terribly early start. I'll see myself off, John—thanks all the same.'

'But I must see you before you go. What about dinner this evening?'

She chewed her lip. Damn Uncle James for putting her in this impossible position. 'All right,' she agreed reluctantly. 'But it will have to be fairly brief, if you don't mind. I'll have to be up very early in the morning.'

The dinner had been a miserable failure. She had been uneasy and preoccupied, whilst John had been touchy and suspicious, putting her more on the defensive than before. They had eaten at a quiet restaurant on the outskirts of Cirencester and when he had taken her home John had hinted that he might come up to her flat to 'say goodbye properly', as he put it. When she had refused he had grown angry.

'Look, just what is going on, Danielle?' he demanded.

She had stared at him in dismay, her heart quickening with apprehension. 'Nothing is *going* on. I don't know what you mean.'

'You're so cool and distant,' he complained. 'And you hardly touched your dinner. Just what *is* this so-called errand of yours?'

'I can't tell you. It's confidential,' she told him miserably.

He sighed. 'I don't know about you, Danielle. Ever since this take-over thing you've been different.'

'Surely you can understand that it's been a difficult time for me. I'll be all right once it's over,' she told him. 'Once I'm away from here and everything is finalised. You'll see.'

She despised herself for the pleading, ingratiating note in her voice. Since this business began her whole life had changed. And what was about to take place would have a lasting effect on her. Of that one thing at least she was sure. Nothing would ever be the same again after Switzerland. She was about to force herself into the arms of a man who would obviously take advantage of the situation—she already knew that from her past experience of Adam Scott's behaviour. The trouble was, that whilst to him it would be nothing more than a pleasant interlude, to her it could well mean heartbreak. Would she be able to return to normal afterwards—marry John as though Adam Scott had never featured in her life? Deep inside she knew the answer was no. But that was something she would have to face when she came to it.

With all these thoughts in her head she had put her arms round John and clung to him. 'Just try to be patient with me,' she whispered.

His kiss had been cool. 'I am trying, Danielle,' he told her stiffly. 'But there are limits.'

The voice that came over the public address system brought Danielle suddenly back to the present and she rose hurriedly, picking up her hand luggage and making sure that she had her boarding pass before setting off on the first stage of her journey.

The flight was uneventful. She collected her luggage and went through Customs, boarding the bus waiting to take passengers to the railway station. As she looked out of the window at the picturesque, medieval architecture of the beautiful old city, she wished that the circumstances could have been different so that she could have enjoyed it all as it deserved to be enjoyed.

She ate lunch on the train, looking wistfully out over Lake Zurich and wishing that she had someone to share its beauty with. She changed trains at a sleepy little halt, and then again at another. Then began the climb into the mountains, along little rocky tracks hewn out of the mountainside, steep drops on one side, rugged, rocky walls on the other. She watched with wonder as farmers worked in fields that seemed to slope quite impossibly steeply; admired the wooden chalets that looked like toy musical boxes with their painted shutters and carved woodwork.

Rocking sleepily in the rambling little train she thought about Adam. She had avoided him ever since Uncle James had told her of his plan, afraid that she might give the whole thing away just by looking into those direct dark eyes. She hardly dared to think of the days ahead—let alone make any kind of plan.

Seduction simply wasn't her line—especially the seduction of a man who was as obviously experienced as Adam. Surely he would see through her; would merely laugh at her? Was she about to fail hopelessly and make a prize fool of herself? She closed her eyes tightly, not daring to accept the possibility of failure; knowing that James Denver expected—would tolerate, nothing less than positive success.

Regansbad was a delight. A little spa town, high in the mountains, that had been a favourite health resort since Victorian times. But by the time Danielle arrived she was too tired, both physically and mentally, to take in its charms. As she drove to the hotel in a taxi she numbly registered the spotlessly clean streets and quaint churches with tall, slender spires; the sparkle of a distant lake, glimpsed occasionally—and all dominated by majestic, snow-capped peaks.

She checked into the hotel and unpacked in the pretty room with its carved golden pine doors and bed-head. She glanced longingly at the high bed with its enormous white duvet and eventually gave in to its beckoning softness, creeping under the fluffy warmth to fall asleep instantly.

When she woke it was time for dinner and Danielle realised that she was hungry. As she showered she wondered whether Adam had arrived yet. As she came back from the bathroom her eye fell on the telephone by the bed and she paused, her hand hovering over it. Then she made up her mind and snatched up the receiver. When the receptionist answered she enquired and was told that—'No, Herr Scott had not arrived yet. Did she wish to be informed when he did?'

Her heart missed a beat at the very thought. 'Oh no—no, thank you. It's all right,' she stammered.

'When he does arrive do you wish me to advise Herr Scott that you are here, Fraulein?' the receptionist asked helpfully.

'No, I—it's to be a—a surprise.' Danielle felt her face colouring as she said it, even though no one could see her. She wished now she hadn't bothered to enquire. The girl would think she was idiotic.

At the other end of the line the voice 'smiled' 'Ah—I see. Of course, I understand, Fraulein. It shall be between ourselves.'

Danielle dropped the receiver back onto its rest, feeling more foolish than before. But one thing at least was a relief. She would be able to eat her dinner in peace!

She was early. The glass doors of the dining room were still closed. Through them she could see the gleaming white tablecloths, laid with impeccable silver; each round table with its own small vase of flowers. The room was richly furnished in turquoise, white and gold and lit by three glittering chandeliers. A diminutive Maitre d'hotel was fussily

111

inspecting his team of waiters, dashing backwards and forwards like a busy little terrier, tweaking a bow tie here and flicking imaginary specks of dust from shoulders with a spotless napkin. Danielle smiled as she watched him, thinking of her own staff at The Royalty and especially Arthur. She had telephoned him before she had left. Explaining to him where she was going hadn't been easy. She had always found it impossible to lie to Arthur, even as a small child. When she had finished her stumbling fabrication there had been a pause, then he had said in a deeply troubled voice:

'You're in some kind of difficulty aren't you, Danny?'

'No! Of course not, Arthur.' She tried to laugh, but even to her own ears it sounded hollow and unconvincing.

'Just tell me one thing: Does it have anything to do with me?'

'No. I can promise you that,' she had assured him.

He gave an audible sigh of relief. 'You say your uncle is sending you abroad for a few days. Are you going alone?'

'Yes—well, no, not exactly. Look, Arthur, don't worry. I'm all right and I'll come and see you when I get back—okay?'

'There's something here I don't like,' he said uneasily. 'Look, Danielle—you don't have to do anything you don't want to. If you're worried come right over here and tell me about it now, while there's still time.'

'I'm fine, Arthur. I'll see you when I get back. Goodbye.' She had put the phone down firmly, then lifted it again and left it off the hook so that he couldn't ring back. She couldn't cope with further complications.

The dining room doors opened and she was ushered to her table. She ate a delicious meal and then returned to her room to settle down to an early night. Tomorrow she was going to need all her wits about her!

She woke early and got out of bed to open the shutters. Outside the air was cold and crystal clear. The view beyond her window took her breath away. Below, the little town lay spread like something from a Disney film with its pretty chalets and churches, but all round, for as far as she could see, the mountains crowded, their snow-covered peaks rosy pink with the glow of the rising sun. A church bell began to toll in the distance, the sound hanging, round, sweet and golden as a ripe apple on the clear air.

Danielle opened the window and leaned out, taking a deep breath. It seemed to sparkle like champagne. No pollution here; no traffic fumes or industrial fug. No wonder it made her feel slightly light-headed.

Downstairs in the dining room she was served by the same waiter as last night. He was young and blond, solicitous and soft-footed, anticipating her every need. And he spoke perfect English. The service here couldn't be faulted, surely, even by Adam himself? The coffee was hot and fragrant, the croissant crisp and there was an impressive selection of small pots of delicious jam. Danielle was just finishing the last morsel when a shadow fell across the sunlit table.

'What the *hell* are you doing here?'

She looked up and her eyes met Adam's. Instantly her cheeks flooded with hot colour and she found herself choking helplessly over a crumb that went down the wrong way.

'I—I'm here to work for you,' she spluttered when she found her voice. 'Uncle James asked me to come. He said that he had other work for Bobby.'

'I'll *bet* he has!' Adam glared at her resentfully, his eyes dark, with annoyance. 'What good did he think *you'd* be to me?' he demanded rudely.

She stared up at him, momentarily lost for words. Obviously he was bitterly disappointed—had been looking forward to spending some time at Regansbad alone with Bobby Hayward. His obvious dismay at finding her here instead wasn't a very good start to what she was there to achieve! But this fact was submerged by her resentment. The injustice of his attitude made her see red.

'Well! Don't bother to *thank* me for stepping into the breach, will you!' she exclaimed, getting to her feet. 'I do happen to have had a full secretarial training. But of course if you can't bear the thought of having me work for you, I'll catch the next plane home!'

Her green eyes flashed with anger as she stood looking up at him. For a moment his expression darkened dangerously, then his lips twitched and suddenly he laughed. Out of the corner of her eye, Danielle saw two waiters who stood nearby, watching them. One nudged the other and they smiled knowingly at each other. She glanced around, biting her lip in anguish as she realised how loudly she had spoken. Had anyone else overheard their confrontation? Adam took her arm firmly and steered her out of the dining room.

'I think we'll continue this conversation somewhere less public,' he said with a wry grin. 'I don't fancy being punched on the nose in front of a dining room full of people. We don't want to get thrown out at this stage in the proceedings, do we?'

The south side of the hotel had a wide, glass-covered terrace running the length of it; furnished with small tables shaded by gaily-striped umbrellas. At that time in the morning it was empty and it was here that Adam steered her, one hand still firmly under her elbow. Pushing her into one of the chairs he looked down at her.

'Would you like some more coffee?'

'No, thank you,' she said, tight-lipped.

'Well, I would if you don't mind. I haven't had my breakfast yet!' He disappeared for a moment, then returned to sit opposite her at the table.

He seemed more relaxed now and the fresh air and magnificent view had a calming effect on Danielle too. For the first time she looked at him properly. He was wearing casual clothes, light brown linen slacks and an open-necked shirt of a rich cream colour which complemented his dark colouring perfectly.

'Wh-when did you arrive?' she asked, haltingly.

'Late last night,' he told her. 'No one told me you were here. James simply said he'd "arranged for a temp". I had no idea—' His eyes narrowed again. 'Just what is he up to?'

'He asked me to fill in, that's all.' She hoped she sounded convincing. 'He thought I'd enjoy a change, I think.' She looked him full in the eyes. 'Anyway, at least I know the hotel business. Surely better me than someone completely strange?'

'Oh, I agree . . .' A waiter arrived with a tray containing a large pot of coffee, croissants and two cups. When he had withdrawn, Adam poured coffee for them both and passed her a cup.

'Here—drink this. You look as though you could do with it. Look, I'm sorry if I seemed unwelcoming. It was just the shock, seeing you

116

sitting there in the dining room when I came down.'

She sipped gratefully at the coffee. How on earth was she supposed to seduce a man who seemed so dismayed at the sight of her? 'I'm sorry that the sight of me was so shattering for you,' she remarked dryly.

He laughed. 'Oh dear, I'm not expressing myself too well this morning, am I?'

She looked at him. 'Well, when and where do we start?'

He shrugged. 'As soon as I've finished breakfast—if you don't mind waiting for me, that is.'

She ignored the small sarcasm. They sat in silence for a moment. 'This is a beautiful hotel,' Danielle said conversationally. 'I don't think you'll find much to improve on here. The service is . . .'

'Oh, *this* isn't the place we're here to look at,' he told her.

She stared at him. 'It isn't? Then where . . . ?'

'I'm surprised that James didn't put you in the picture more thoroughly while he was about it,' he told her. 'No. We already own this place. What I'm here to look at is a smallish lodge halfway up that mountain there.' He pointed. 'The idea is to develop it into a ski centre, a very exclusive one. It's quite an old building, in the traditional Swiss style, which is what makes it so attractive. At the moment it's

117

being used as a restaurant. I'm here to decide whether it's a viable proposition or not—to assess what it would cost to convert and work out the economics.'

She smiled. As far as the work went, her stay here should be interesting. 'It sounds fascinating,' she said.

'Right then.' He stood up. 'I'm glad you approve. We'll make a start, shall we?'

They began their journey in the funicular, then changed for a cable-car. Danielle looked down, watching the climbers on the lower slopes, tiny specks among the bright green grass that was still studded with patches of snow, as well as the masses of purple and white flowers that grew in wild profusion. Adam surprised her by dropping an arm suddenly over her shoulders as he looked down with her.

'Breathtaking, isn't it?'

She nodded. 'I've never been to Switzerland before—always wanted to.' She laughed. 'Odd when you think that this time last week I hadn't a clue I'd be coming.'

He smiled thoughtfully into her upturned face. 'I must try to remember not to work you too hard. You should have time to stand and stare a little, your first time here.'

The lodge was quite beautiful, rustic and picturesque; a place where climbers or sight-seers could rest on their journey up or down the mountain. Its position was perfect for a ski centre and, as they sat drinking coffee on a balcony that seemed suspended breathlessly out over the precipice, Adam explained some of the alterations that would need to be made and the skill required in executing them so as not to spoil the old building.

They met Herr Fixl, the elderly owner. A jovial little man with white hair and a busy moustache. He was as round as a barrel, but brisk and businesslike as he toured the building with them, explaining everything as they went. Adam asked endless questions, the answers to which Danielle noted carefully, hoping feverishly that she would be able to read her rather rusty shorthand later when she came to type it all out into a report. The owner invited them to take lunch with him, which they did before making the return journey.

During the afternoon they visited an architect Adam had had recommended to him. He lived in a beautiful house he had designed for himself. It jutted out over one of the lower slopes in what seemed to Danielle a miracle of engineering and was, inside, the perfect mixture of modern and traditional design. Danielle was fascinated as he showed them round, then sat them down to tea and delicious cream pastries served by his wife whilst he and Adam settled down to discuss possible ideas for the lodge. As they talked Danielle realised just how much work there was still to do. There would be craftsmen and builders to interview and a hundred other things to think about. Their work could last many days yet!

That evening Adam and Herr Fixl dined together. Danielle excused herself and ate alone in her room, grateful to escape. Afterwards she worked until late, typing up the report of the day's findings. It was only when she had finally finished and went to run a bath to ease her aching muscles that she remembered the real reason for her being here and her heart sank. Today had been so full, so packed with interest, that she had completely forgotten her mission. It was time she thought seriously about how she was to accomplish what she was here for!

Lying in the warm water, she felt her stomach churn with apprehension. The more she saw of Adam, the more inexperienced and immature she felt. What chance had she against a man who knew his way around as he did? He would see through her in a moment. She pictured him laughing at her transparent and faltering attempts to snare him. It was *ludicrous*!

She climbed out of the bath and wrapped herself in a towel, gazing at her reflection in the mirror. Terrified green eyes looked back at her, still shocked at the images she had created. It was no use, she told herself. She simply couldn't do it. Uncle James would just have to do his worst!

CHAPTER SEVEN

The two days that followed were as full as the first and, now that Danielle had made up her mind not to attempt her uncle's mission, she found it was possible to enjoy herself. Adam treated her impersonally. She might have been a temporary secretary from the agency and she was grateful for it. Almost rushed off her feet, there was no time to ponder on her personal feelings towards him. Even in her rare moments of quiet her thoughts lingered only briefly on her reason for being here. Adam's sheer dynamism made her head spin and by the end of each day she was so exhausted that she fell asleep almost as soon as her head touched the pillow. She found it stimulating and exciting and she had to admit that keeping pace with him gave her a sense of achievement.

Each of the three evenings he had dined with someone associated with the project, whilst she had eaten alone in her room and then spent the evening typing up the day's work on the portable machine supplied by the hotel. But when she came down to breakfast on the fourth morning she found Adam waiting for her in a relaxed mood. As usual she handed him the folder containing the previous day's notes and data, all neatly typed and collated. He took it from her with a smile as she sat down at the table.

'Thank you, Danielle.' He watched her pour her coffee, taking in the new incandescent glow she had acquired since she had been in Regansbad; admiring the light, golden tan the mountain air had given her complexion and the new sparkle in her eyes. As she looked up he averted his eyes, opening the folder and examining the notes briefly.

'Well—that's that!' he said suddenly, slapping the folder down on the table.

'What's the matter? Did I do something wrong?' she asked, startled.

'You certainly did not!' He looked at her solemnly. 'I confess that I misjudged you, Danielle. I thought you wouldn't be up to this job—that you'd wilt at the pace I like to do things, but you've proved me wrong. You've been marvellous.'

She took a sip of her coffee, avoiding his eyes and hoping he wouldn't notice her warm blush of pleasure. Compliments were almost as hard to take from him as insults. 'I did tell you I'd had a good training,' she muttered ungraciously. 'Well, what do we do today?'

He smiled. 'We take a holiday.'

Her eyes opened wide with dismay. Working together was one thing—being alone with him for a whole day without the stout barrier of work between them was something else. 'A holiday?' She swallowed, trying to keep the

122

note of panic out of her. 'But you said you wanted to see the bank manager about the transfer . . .'

His hand shot out to cover hers as she fiddled nervously with the butter knife. 'I said a lot of things—and you're right, there is still a lot to be done. It's just that I think we deserve a day off. You don't object to that, do you?'

She shook her head. What could she say? 'Of course not. Wh-what did you have in mind?' she enquired nervously.

He laughed. 'No need to sound so apprehensive. I'm not about to lure you to some sinister castle and introduce you to the Swiss equivalent of Count Dracula. I thought to begin with we'd *walk* up a mountain instead of riding in the cable car.' He smiled. 'Don't look so panic-stricken. I don't mean right to the summit! You'd be surprised what a lot there is to see. As I said the other day, on your first trip to Switzerland you should take time out to "stand and stare".' He smiled. 'I've ordered a picnic lunch. Is that to your liking?'

'Well—if you're really sure we can spare the time—it sounds very nice,' she said with growing unease.

Half an hour later they left the hotel dressed in jeans and anoraks, Adam carrying the rucksacks containing their picnic. For the first time Danielle realised that Regansbad was built like a series of terraces, the streets tiered, one above the other.

'Everywhere you go there is the sound of running water,' she remarked as they walked.

Adam nodded. 'Gullies run under each street to allow the water from the mountain springs to run down into the lake,' he told her. 'Of course, in winter it's all frozen. There's skating on the lake and the mountains are full of skiers. It's a great place to be then.'

As they walked the steep mountain paths Danielle saw that everything was blossoming. Everywhere there were wild flowers and new green leaves. They crossed a rustic bridge under which a stream bubbled over a rocky bed. But for all the beauty all around her Danielle could not relax. She felt awkward and tongue-tied, her thoughts constantly playing on the real reason for her being here. She couldn't help reflecting that if she had still intended to carry it out this would have been a heaven-sent opportunity.

They had been walking for some time when they came to the ravine. Below them the little town lay like a scattering of bright jewels, surrounded by magnificent scenery. The air was exhilarating and they stopped to take a breather and to look into the deep gorge where a sparkling ribbon of water fell some forty feet into a rocky pool below. Adam eased the straps of the rucksack over his arms and lowered it to the ground, smiling at her.

'I'd say this was a perfect place for lunch, wouldn't you?'

She nodded. 'It's beautiful.'

They unpacked the lunch provided by the hotel and Adam attacked it with relish. Danielle had no appetite, picking at the delicious food without enthusiasm. Adam looked at her in surprise.

'Not hungry—and after all that healthy exercise and mountain air?'

'Not very.' She rose and walked across to gaze down into the rocky crevice, watching the gleaming strand of water as it dropped dizzily into the pool below; the sunlight catching the flying droplets and turning them into diamonds.

'I feel like that,' she told herself. 'Plunging endlessly—unable to help myself.' Suddenly her spirits plummeted as she faced the fact that she must return to Britain with her uncle's plan unfulfilled. She wondered what he would do and what madness had ever made her agree to it. Adam Scott was his own man. He may have amused himself with her but she hadn't the power to persuade him to turn from whatever it was he had decided he wanted from life. Sheer desperation must have fooled her into thinking she could. When she returned she faced certain bankruptcy and the loss of The Royalty. But that wasn't all. Before Adam came into her life she had been content and happy. But he had lifted a veil for her—given her a glimpse of a whole world of experience she had never dreamed of. How was she to pick up the threads of her life again? She swallowed hard at the lump in her throat but her eyes filled with tears, blurring the view before her.

'Is anything wrong?' He had joined her silently and stood behind her.

'Why are we here?' she asked, without turning. 'Oh, I know what you *said*—but we should be working when there is so much to do.'

He took her arm and swung her round to face him. 'Why is it that every damn thing I do is suspect . . .' He broke off, his eyes narrowing as he saw the tears on her cheeks. 'What is it? What's the matter?'

She drew a deep breath and dashed the tears away angrily with the back of her hand. 'It's nothing,' she told him huskily, pushing past him and returning to the lunch spread out on the ground. As she began to pack the remains into the rucksack he came up behind her.

'All right, Danielle. You win. I admit I did have an ulterior motive for this outing. And it's odd you should ask that question. I asked you out for the day to find out the real reason behind your being here. I'm not a fool, you know.'

She felt as though an icy hand had closed round her heart. Momentarily she stopped what she was doing, then, taking a deep breath she continued pushing the lunch things into

126

the bag.

'I don't know what you mean. I came out here to take the place of your personal assistant—because Uncle James needed her for something else,' she told him slowly and deliberately. 'I thought that was clear. I . . .'

'Danielle—stop it!' He grasped her shoulders and drew her to her feet, then turned her round to face him, his eyes searching hers. 'Now let's have the truth— why? Why *you*, I mean. There's a perfectly good "temp" agency we've used a dozen times, so why did James ask you to come? And, what's more to the point—why did you agree? After all, our relationship so far has hardly been what you might call friendly, has it?'

She forced herself to meet the probing eyes. 'All right. I admit that I've been difficult most of the time. You saved the day for me on the day you sacked Arthur—even if you were mistaken over it, I was grateful and . . .'

He shook his head impatiently. 'Don't be such a bloody little hypocrite! You're not grateful at all! And anyway, that still wouldn't explain your uncle's reason for asking you.'

Danielle felt like a mouse in a trap. She cast about feverishly in her mind for a reasonable excuse. 'How should *I* know why he asked me?' she snapped defensively. 'Perhaps he thought the trip would do me good. He *is* my uncle don't forget. Maybe he realised that I've had a traumatic time lately.'

His lips curled sardonically. 'Forgive me, but that doesn't sound much like the James Denver I know!'

'Perhaps you underestimate him.' She shrugged and made to turn away but he caught her by the shoulders, gripping her tightly as he asked: 'In that case, why are you so ill at ease with me today?'

Inside her the tension stretched unbearably, taut as a violin string. She wanted to scream and lash out at him physically but she bit the inside of her lip and made herself look into his eyes. 'Perhaps you should ask yourself that, Adam. As you say, we haven't exactly hit it off together since we met, have we?'

'We've worked well enough together for the last three days.'

'Then maybe that's how we should keep it,' she said crisply. 'As a *working* relationship.' She lifted her hands to free herself from his grasp and suddenly his eyes fell on her left hand. He caught at it, holding it fast.

'Does this have something to do with it, Danielle?' When she didn't answer he shook her gently, making it clear that he was not going to let her go until she answered his question. 'Tell me where your engagement ring is,' he persisted.

Warm colour flooded her cheeks. She had almost forgotten the ring she had discarded on her uncle's instructions before flying out to Switzerland. Staring numbly at her ringless left

128

hand, she said: 'I—it's over—John and I.' Shock waves hit her as she realised that what she was saying was true. She knew it now. She couldn't marry John. It was out of the question. She had known it for some time really—perhaps even before Adam arrived at Kingswood.

His eyes searched hers. 'I'm sorry. I had no right to question you like that.' He looked at her with a wry smile. 'So you're running away! You must be desperate, Danielle, if you chose *my* company!'

She shook her head wearily. 'Adam, please—I don't want to talk about it.'

He dropped his hands to his sides. 'I might have known. I told myself you were too obsessed with that damned hotel ever to leave it without good reason. But under the circumstances . . .' He frowned. 'But why the secrecy? Why didn't you just say when I asked you?'

'I don't have to tell you everything about my personal life, do I?' she snapped indignantly. 'Even if you do put me through the third degree!'

He laughed. 'That's more like the Danielle I know. Well—how about this day off we're supposed to be having? There's still more than half of it left!'

She returned to packing the rucksack, wondering how she would possibly get through the rest of the day. 'I don't think I'm really in the mood. You go.'

'Rubbish!' He hauled her to her feet. 'Come on. We're going back to the hotel to change. I'll give you one hour!'

One look at the determined set of his mouth told her there was little point in arguing with him.

An hour later Danielle found herself sitting beside Adam in a hired car, driving along narrow mountain roads towards Liechtenstein. As she stared in wonder at the breathtaking scenery she was grateful for the diversion it provided. Adam, who had obviously been here many times before, pointed out places of interest on the way: the towering Seven Sisters mountain range and the narrow bubbling river they crossed, which to her surprise she learned was no less than the great Rhine.

The tiny Principality of Liechtenstein was a delight. A fairytale place that looked as though it had been built as the setting for a musical film. Sitting under the colourful awning of a pavement cafe, Danielle could see the Schloss Vaduz high on the wooded mountain shelf where it dominated the town. Its rose-coloured multi-shaped rooftops dreamed in the sunshine against a backcloth of towering snow-capped peaks.

Adam watched her, smiling a little. She was appealingly childlike as she stared up at it all, wide-eyed with delight. 'Fantastic, isn't it?' he said.

She looked across at him, their differences forgotten for the moment. 'Unbelievably beautiful.'

'Glad you came now?'

She lowered her eyes. 'I wouldn't have missed seeing this. Thank you.'

'And this evening . . . ? I know a place where they still have authentic Swiss entertainment, not just tourist stuff, and it's almost on the doorstep of the hotel. We won't even need a car.'

She opened her mouth to make an excuse, then closed it again, knowing that he had no intention of taking no for an answer. He seemed determined to entertain her. Perhaps in his own fashion he was trying to make up for the way they had clashed in the past. It would be ungracious of her to refuse. Somehow she must get through it. She made herself smile. 'Thank you. It sounds very nice.'

They arrived back at the hotel as the sun was going down. Danielle lay in the bath, her eyes closed. The whole day had been an ordeal for her. She remembered with a sinking heart the way her senses had stirred at Adam's touch—the way his nearness disturbed her. She had thought she was getting through their stay here quite well, she told herself ironically. Today had been nothing short of sheer torment—and she still had this evening to face. Short of sudden illness there was no way she could avoid it.

She dressed slowly, trying not to let her mind dwell on the coming hours. She chose a dress of soft jersey silk in a silvery green shade that flattered her colouring. It was quite plain except for narrow diamante straps. She swept her hair up into a smooth coronet, securing it with a matching circlet of diamante, the only jewellery she wore. They ate dinner together for the first time since she had been in Switzerland. Adam was in a relaxed mood, ordering all the dishes he knew the chef excelled in and insisting that she drank her share of the sparkling white wine he ordered to go with it.

The Postil was almost next door to the hotel. It was built in the old Swiss style, its exterior decorated with brightly painted murals depicting the old way of life. Inside, it was decorated with quaint local carving and more traditional paintings. The tables were laid with checked cloths and in the centre of each a candle burned in its little glass holder. A small band was playing with more enthusiasm than musical skill, the musicians dressed in colourful, informal clothes.

Adam ordered a bottle of wine and they watched as the place filled up with local people, out to enjoy themselves for the evening. As the time went by and the atmosphere grew more and more relaxed the music grew louder to rise above the noise of laughter and happy voices. People got up to

132

dance and there were one or two impromptu displays of dancing and singing which had them both laughing. Slowly, Danielle felt herself beginning to relax in the happy atmosphere, a feeling of euphoria took over. Why not enjoy herself? she asked. After all, once she got home there would be nothing but problems to face. Adam's face across the table began to look kinder, less forbidding. The wine crept into her bones, dissolving her fears and inhibitions.

After a time the lights were lowered until only the candlelight illuminated the room. The music became softer, the dancing less frenetic. Adam looked at Danielle enquiringly, rising from the table and holding out his hand. She rose reluctantly to her feet, her heart quickening a little at the thought of being held in his arms again. But the wine she had consumed blurred the edges of her apprehension, making her feel mellow and languorous.

On the tiny floor it was impossible to take up too much room and the arm that encircled her waist drew her close. Through the thin silk of her dress she could feel the warmth of his hand on her back. The taut muscles of his thighs pressed against hers as they moved together and her senses began to reel. The hand that clasped hers drew her arm in until it was resting against his chest and presently he left it there to slide his left arm round her, his fingers spreading against her back, crushing her against him. The cheek that rubbed against hers was warm and smooth and as he spoke she felt his breath fan her ear tantalisingly.

'Well—are you glad you came now?' His voice was low and husky.

There was a slight catch in her voice as she whispered, 'Yes—very glad. Thank you Adam.'

He raised his head to look down at her. 'No regrets?'

She wasn't quite sure what he meant, but she smiled dreamily, shaking her head then resting it against his shoulder with a sigh. She felt a slight tremor go through him and his hand came round to lift her chin, tipping her face up towards his. She caught a brief glimpse of dark, smouldering eyes before his mouth came down on hers.

She felt as though she were suspended, her feet hardly touching the floor as they moved together, their lips brushing; asking unspoken questions—giving answers that spoke louder than words. She closed her eyes, her heart racing as his lips finally claimed hers in a long sensuous kiss. Somewhere deep inside a small voice told her this was madness, that she would be sure to regret it. But other, more powerful, emotions took her over and the voice was silenced.

'Is it really true?' he asked her. 'Is your engagement really over?'

She gave him an almost imperceptible nod

and felt his arm tighten round her in response.

'Tell me the truth, Danielle—did the reason have anything to do with me?' His eyes were dark as she looked up into them and whispered:

'Yes.'

'Let's go,' he whispered in her ear. She went with him, moving as though in a dream, her hand clinging to his as she followed him out into the cool, crisp night air.

High above, the moon and a million stars seemed to burn with a clear, brilliant light she had never seen before. She gazed up at them as Adam paused to wrap her soft white angora shawl around her shoulders, brushing his lips briefly across her forehead as he did so.

It was late and they tiptoed hand-in-hand past the dozing night porter and sped upwards in the lift, Adam's hand still holding hers tightly. He took her key from her and opened the door. Inside, in a darkness lit only by the moonlight coming through the open window, she turned instinctively into his open arms. All her inhibitions were gone. All thoughts of Britain, The Royalty and the problems it entailed were swept away in the need that seemed to ravish her very soul.

Adam's lips claimed hers, kissing her till her head swam dizzily. He pulled the pins from her hair till it tumbled about her shoulders, tangling his fingers in its thick richness as though to imprison her. When his mouth left hers he bent to press his lips into the hollow of her throat, pausing against the little pulse that fluttered there before moving on to taste the smooth flesh of her bare shoulder. His arms crushed her urgently against him, one hand hard against the small of her back, straining her to him. Then he was slipping the diamante straps from her shoulders, his fingers unzipping her dress. As it fell with a soft rustle about her feet she let her head fall back in abandon, her lips parted and her eyes closed as she felt his strong arms sweep her feet from the ground and put her gently down on the bed.

He took her face between his hands, kissing her lips, her cheeks, her eyelids, murmuring her name over and over.

'I love you,' she heard herself whispering as she drowned in his kisses. 'I love you, Adam.'

He lifted his head to look down at her. 'Shhh. Don't you know that you should never bare your soul like that to any man?' Tenderly he brushed a strand of hair from her forehead. 'Dear God, Danielle. You're so lovely,' he whispered. He ran a hand down the length of her body and felt a ripple of ecstasy go through her. 'I think you know how much I want you, don't you?'

She looked up at him, her eyes luminous in the dim light. 'I want you too.'

He looked at her for a long moment, his eyes suddenly clouding, then he withdrew from her suddenly, reaching for the duvet and covering her with it. Her eyes looked up at him, huge and suddenly afraid.

'What's wrong?' she asked in a whisper. 'What have I done?'

He sat silently on the edge of the bed for a moment, his back towards her, his head in his hands, then he turned and said: 'I never thought I'd hear myself say a thing like this, but I can't—It would be taking advantage and it's too important to spoil, Danielle. I think you know that.'

She sat up and reached out for him, her heart beating unevenly. 'I told you, Adam I lo . . .'

He covered her lips with his fingers, shaking his head at her. 'No—don't say it. Not now.' There was a hint of wistfulness in his smile as he added: 'Darling—you've had an awful lot of wine.'

She reached out to him as he made to get up. 'That has nothing to do with it. Don't go, Adam—please!'

He turned, bending to kiss her, raising her face to his and looking into her eyes. 'Don't make it harder, darling. If I stayed—if I allowed it to happen you'd hate me tomorrow and believe me, Danielle, that's the very last thing I want.' He cupped her face. 'I'll wait for you to say it again when I'm sure you know what you're saying. And I hope—oh, I *hope* you'll mean it.'

She closed her eyes. Deep inside she knew

137

at that moment that she had never meant anything more—that she would have given him her very soul if he'd asked for it. But he hadn't. He couldn't want her as she wanted him. In some way she must have disappointed him.

Sensing her thoughts he pulled her close, his voice ragged as he said: 'Listen. There's something I want you to know, Danielle. You've probably guessed that I've had a good many women friends—relationships, but there has never been anyone remotely like you.'

She pulled away, not quite able to believe him, and he took her chin, his fingers hard and insistent against her jawbone as they dragged her face round. 'Look at me! I *mean* it. If I hadn't felt that I would have taken advantage of you without a second thought. Can't you see that?'

A dozen questions rose to her lips. She longed to ask him about his relationship with Bobby. After all, it had been serious enough to arouse his stepfather's concern. He looked into her uncertain eyes and pulled her to him again.

'You know as well as I do that it's been there between us since the moment we set eyes on each other, this attraction. It has—hasn't it?' he demanded. 'Drawing us to each other like a magnet. Admit it, Danielle!' He gave her a wry smile. 'Damn it, I had my work cut out keeping away from you right from the first. You know that, and I believe you felt the same, even though you may not have read it that way at first. Now we both know it's more than just an attraction, don't we?'

She nodded, reaching out to touch his face. 'Yes, that's true.'

He caught at the hand that touched his cheek, turning his lips into the palm. When he looked at her again his eyes were passionate in their sincerity. 'And that's exactly why I'm going to leave you now.' He bent and kissed her swiftly. 'I'll see you in the morning,' he whispered. 'Sweet dreams my love. Tomorrow we'll talk—start afresh.'

Lying in bed, she watched as he hastily put on his jacket, loving with her eyes the strong, rippling muscles and the tanned skin, the broad shoulders and the proud set of his head. She wanted to belong to him more than she had ever wanted anything in her whole life, but she hardly dared hope such happiness could really be hers. Deep inside she was suddenly frightened. Impulsively she jumped up, wrapping her dressing gown around her. Standing on tiptoe she put her arms around his neck and kissed him.

'Nothing can change, Adam,' she promised. 'I'll feel the same tomorrow—and all the other tomorrows.'

'I've waited half a lifetime for a girl like you,' he told her huskily. 'So I hope you're right.'

After he had gone she lay for a long time, thinking drowsily. Tomorrow she would tell him the truth about her reason for being here—explain her desperation in accepting her uncle's plan and her utter failure in carrying it out. She would ask him about Bobby too. Everything between them must be honest and clear-cut. Only then would she feel free to love him. With a pang she remembered John and her half-lie about their engagement. She had no wish to hurt John, especially after his goodness to her. But the moment she got back home she must see him—try somehow to make him see that marriage between them could never have worked.

*   *   *

She woke to a tap on the door. Sleepily she pulled herself upright, blinking against the strong sunlight that streamed into the room. She called: 'Come in.'

The door opened and Adam came in carrying a tray. 'I ordered breakfast in bed for you,' he told her with a smile. 'I had an idea you might be feeling a little frail. I've got aspirins too, if you want them.'

She shook her head, smoothing her hair self-consciously, wondering what she must look like. 'I feel fine,' she told him. It was true. She had never felt so marvellous in her life in spite of all the problems that lay before her. Somehow she knew with a sudden surge of joy that if Adam really loved her anything was

140

possible.

'You look it too.' He set the tray across her legs and sat on the edge of the bed. He wore a bathrobe and as he bent forward to kiss her she saw that he still had pyjamas on underneath it.

'I caught the maid in the corridor,' he explained, reading her thoughts. 'I was waiting for her. I wanted to bring it to you myself.'

Danielle smiled at him and looked at the tray. The fragrance of freshly-made coffee tempted her appetite. 'Thank you,' she said. 'It was a lovely thought. But I'll get up as soon as I've eaten it. We have a lot to do.'

'And to talk about,' he reminded her. 'But there's no hurry. Take your time.' He stood up. 'I'll go and finish dressing. See you soon.'

She poured herself a cup of coffee and was just spreading butter on a croissant when there was another tap on the door. She called 'Come in,' but when nothing happened she pushed aside the tray and got out of bed, pulling on her dressing gown. She opened the door—then gasped with amazement, staring in disbelief at the person waiting outside. A hand shot out to push her unceremoniously back into the room and the door closed firmly with them both on the inside.

John Peterson's face was haggard and his eyes glittered, cold as ice behind the gold-rimmed glasses as he stared at her angrily.

'All right, Danielle. I want to hear all about

141

it in your own words. And you'd better make it the truth this time. I've been travelling all night and I'm in no mood for fairytales!'

She took a step backwards. 'John! I didn't mean to lie to you. I was going to tell you everything . . .'

'Oh, *were* you? Well I'll tell you instead, shall I?' He grasped her shoulders, his fingers biting painfully into her flesh. 'You came here specifically to seduce Scott—you and your uncle planned it between you.' He laughed mirthlessly at the expression on her face. 'Oh yes, I know all about it so you needn't bother to deny it. And if I was in any doubts I've just had the proof. As I got out of the lift just now I saw Scott come out of your room!' His eyes glinted with triumph as he saw her flinch. 'You're doing this to repay your father's debts and let yourself off the hook!' He bent closer to her, his mouth twisted with fury. 'And to think I almost married you—a woman who'd do a thing like that! There's a name for your sort of woman, Danielle.' He bent closer, his angry breath hissing in her ear. 'Do you want me to tell you what it is?'

Before she could reply a voice cut in, a voice as hard and cold as steel: 'That's enough, Peterson. We'll handle this in a civilised way, if you don't mind.'

As John turned, moving to one side, their eyes met—Danielle's frozen with horror—Adam's dark with angry betrayal.

CHAPTER EIGHT

Danielle recoiled as Adam closed the door behind him and advanced slowly and deliberately into the room.

'Just what are you doing here, Peterson?' he asked.

John snorted indignantly. 'Why am *I* here? That's rich! At the risk of sounding melodramatic, I've come to take my fiancée home out of the clutches of two unscrupulous men!'

Adam looked at Danielle. 'Do *you* know what he's talking about?'

She stared at him helplessly, wishing she could wake and find it was all a hideous dream—wishing that some miracle would happen to save her. Just how much had Adam overheard before he had decided to intervene? She opened her mouth without having the slightest idea what she was going to say, but before she could speak John broke in:

'Were you aware of what was being planned for you, Scott? Were you aware that she was being used as *bait* to get you away from what your stepfather described as *an unsuitable relationship*?' He paused to allow the revelation to sink in before he added, with a glance at Danielle's ashen face: 'And *she* went along with it. Know why? Because her father owed his brother money and this was the cheap and easy way to pay off the debt!' He drew a deep breath, looking from one to the other as they stared numbly into each other's eyes. 'A nice girl, isn't she, Scott? With nice relatives! You should thank your lucky stars you're only related to them by marriage!' He stared at Danielle. 'All this is going to take some forgiving on my part, I can tell you!'

Suddenly she found her voice, rounding on him. 'I don't want your forgiveness—yours or anyone's. And it's not the way you make it sound.'

'Then how is it, Danielle?' Adam's voice cut in, cold and clear as the dark eyes that met hers. 'Maybe you owe us both an explanation.'

She crumpled. How *could* she explain? Everything John had said was true theoretically, though God only knew how he had found out. Suddenly her fear and dismay erupted into anger—anger at the way she had been manipulated—at the lack of trust these two men were displaying towards her. Both condemning her before she could speak one word in her own defence.

'Oh—get out!' she shouted exasperatedly at them, her throat tight with angry tears. 'I'm leaving and I want to pack. Go away and leave me alone!'

Adam crossed the room towards her. One hand snaked out to grasp her face, jerking it round to look into her eyes.

'Just tell me one thing,' he hissed. 'What Peterson's just said—is it true?'

She moved her head, trying to avoid the eyes that burned accusingly into hers, wincing as his fingers bruised her jaw. 'I . . .'

'Just one word—*yes or no!*' he barked.

'All right—if you force me—*yes!*'

Helpless tears filled her eyes as he turned abruptly on his heel and left the room, slamming the door behind him. John looked triumphant.

'Right, better get some clothes on and pack as quickly as you can. You and I have a train to catch.'

'I'm not going with you,' she told him miserably. But he wasn't listening. Opening the wardrobe he began to toss her clothes onto the bed.

'Don't argue with me, Danielle. I've already paid your bill. I'm not having *them* pay for you to be here. Get ready. I'm not leaving here without you. You don't want to make a scene, do you?'

She didn't see Adam again before they left. Staring numbly out of the train window she watched the beautiful scenery flash past, unable to believe that only a few hours ago she had enjoyed the same scenery with Adam. The journey to Zurich seemed interminable, but at last they were crossing the city to the airport and boarding the plane. She felt she hardly knew the man who sat beside her. He was behaving more like an outraged Victorian father than a fiance—treating her as though she were an errant child. If she hadn't felt so paralysed with misery she would have found enough spirit to challenge him with it. As it was she just sat, staring unseeingly out at the tarmac as they waited for take-off.

They had exchanged no more than a handful of words on the journey so far, but on the plane he suddenly grew talkative, determined to tell her how he had come to find out about what he called her *exploits*.

'I discovered a few shares your father owned,' he told her. 'Almost worthless but I thought you might like to cash them in. I needed your signature so I brought them along to The Royalty so that you'd see them the moment you returned. Sandra gave me a key so that I could leave them in your room. That was where I noticed this—lying on the dressing table like some *chain store trinket*!' He put his hand in his pocket and produced her engagement ring. She turned her head away but he snatched her hand and forced it back onto her finger.

'I went downstairs and asked to see Scott. To my surprise I was told that *he* was in Switzerland too. That was when I began to smell a rat, so I demanded to speak to your uncle.' He shook his head at her. 'What an unpleasant character *he* turned out to be! He spoke to me as though I had no right to be

146

there—no right to ask where you were and what you were doing—my own fiancée! When I'd given him my own views on the subject he told me the whole story with a sort of sadistic pleasure. I believe he enjoyed it—saw it as a good joke!' He took her hand. 'I tell you, Danielle, the sooner you're married to me and away from that set-up, the happier I'll be.'

'I'm not going to marry you, John,' she told him in a flat voice.

He laughed. 'Don't be absurd, of course you are. You're just sulking now because I've caught you out and made you look foolish, but you'll get over that. Just admit you've done a stupid thing and we'll forget all about it.'

She turned to look at his smug expression. How little he understood her if he really believed what he was saying. 'But you implied at the hotel that you'd had a lucky escape,' she reminded him.

He shrugged dismissively. 'I was angry. What man wouldn't be?' He squeezed her hand. 'We all say things we don't mean. I'm prepared to forgive what you've done, Danielle. I'll put it down to your youth and thoughtlessness. You must promise that in future you'll ask me for help when you're in trouble. You're obviously totally incapable of running your own life.' He smiled indulgently at her. 'Oh yes, I'm sure we shall live this down if we both work at it.'

'I won't!' She turned to look at him, her

mouth stubborn. 'I can just see how it would be, John. Every time I stepped out of line I'd have it thrown in my face. You're the kind of man who'd have no hesitation in using it as a weapon to make me toe the line.' She looked at him. 'Long before any of this happened I had doubts about us, John,' she said as gently as she could. 'I know now that it would never work.'

He stared at her, his face a dull red. 'What the hell do you mean—it wouldn't work?'

'I don't love you,' she told him quietly. 'And what's more, you don't love me. You just want to *own* me.'

The hand that held hers tightened, crushing her fingers painfully as John hissed at her: 'I've never heard such a load of rubbish in my life! Listen to me, Danielle. Not many men would take you back after what you've just been up to. You should think yourself damned lucky to have got away with it. So let's hear no more nonsense.'

An air stewardess who was passing with a trolley of duty-free cigarettes glanced curiously at them and Danielle bit back the reply that was on her lips. This wasn't the time or the place to convince John that their engagement was at an end. It would have to wait until later. Besides, she still had her uncle to face; a task she looked forward to with growing dread.

Looking back afterwards she didn't know how she tolerated the rest of the journey.

Sitting next to John on the plane, and, later, in his car all the way back to Kingswood his attitude made her feel cheap and unclean. When she thought of Adam—of his arms around her—of the things they had said to each other last night her heart filled with tears. She had been right to be afraid that something would happen to spoil it. She thought of him, back there in Switzerland. How he must hate her! He must feel cheated and betrayed and she couldn't blame him. If only she had had the courage to tell him everything last night when she had the chance. If she had she wouldn't be sitting here like this now, her inside knotted with misery and her heart torn with regret.

As they drew up outside The Royalty, John turned to her. 'Do you want me to come in with you?'

She shook her head. Her need to be alone in her own room was an almost physical ache. 'No—thank you.'

'What are you going to do?'

'I don't know. I shall have to talk to Uncle James.'

'You'll be in touch?'

Her nerves at breaking point, she wanted to scream at him to go away and leave her alone. Instead she pulled the ring from her finger. 'No. It's better to end it here and now, John. I told you—it wouldn't work. I've never been more sure of anything in my life.'

He thrust the ring back at her. 'Just because you've let that—that *Casanova* make love to you, you think you're missing out on something!' He spluttered angrily. 'That man must have had more women than you can count! Naturally he took advantage when you threw yourself at him. He'd have taken advantage of anything in a skirt. He's that type. And I've had a taste of the way *you* operate, don't forget, Danielle. Not everyone has my control . . .'

'*Stop it!*' She pressed her hands over her ears. 'Why must you make it all sound so disgusting—so cheap and shoddy? You're *wrong*! Wrong about me and—wrong about everything! As for love—I don't think you know the meaning of the word!' She jumped out of the car, tears streaming down her cheeks. Immediately, John revved the engine furiously and pressed his foot down hard on the accelerator, throwing up a spray of gravel against her legs. It was only as she watched his car hurtling away that she remembered her suitcase, still in the boot.

* * *

'So you're back. It's good to see you looking so well, Danielle.'

She swung round at the sound of her uncle's quiet voice. He stood by the desk in Reception, smiling coolly at her. 'Where is your luggage'?' he asked. 'Is it coming later?'

'I'm afraid I left it in John's car. Can I speak to you, Uncle?'

Sandra was watching from the other side of the desk, her face showing concern for her employer.

'You must be tired after the journey, Miss Denver,' she said. 'Why don't you go up and rest for a while. I'll have some tea sent up for you.'

James Denver smiled his agreement. 'What a good idea. We'll have dinner together this evening, Danielle. You'll feel better once you've rested.'

She was lying on the bed, eyes closed, trying to blot out a situation that was rapidly assuming nightmare proportions, when Sandra came in with a tray. On it was a pot of tea and a plate of thinly-cut sandwiches. She placed it on the bedside table.

'Do try and eat something, Miss Denver,' the girl begged. 'You look worn out.'

Danielle shook her head. 'I couldn't, Sandra.'

The girl drew up a chair and sat down beside the bed. 'I wanted to talk to you. I feel it's my fault that Mr Peterson found out where you were. I don't know what happened—don't want to know, but if I've done something to cause trouble for you . . .'

Danielle opened her eyes and put out a hand to touch Sandra's arm. 'No—it wasn't your fault. I can't explain, Sandra, but I've made a terrible mess of things. I'd better warn you—I may be leaving here tomorrow—for good. If it does come to that I'd be grateful if you'd tell the rest of the staff. I'd probably make a fool of myself if I tried to.' There was a tell-tale catch in her voice as she went on: 'Tell them I'm sorry and I shall miss them all, will you?'

Sandra shook her head, her eyes filling with tears. 'Oh, Miss Denver! Don't talk like that. Surely there's some other way.'

Danielle bit her lip hard. 'No, Sandra,' she said bleakly. 'I'm very much afraid there won't be.'

Dinner with Uncle James was an ordeal she dreaded, but she didn't intend to allow it to pass without telling him her own side of things.

'I have to admit that I failed, Uncle,' she told him as they reached the coffee stage. 'I don't think I could have done what you asked, but you hardly helped, telling John my whereabouts and what my mission was. He was quite understandably angry and Adam overheard everything he said to me when he arrived this morning.'

James Denver shook his head, concentrating on the cigar he was lighting. 'Never mind. It achieved part of my aim. I wanted Adam out of the way for a few extra days and it worked. By the way . . .' He looked up at her casually, 'how did the project go?'

152

She stared at him disbelievingly. He had lit a fuse under her future, watched it go up like a keg of gunpowder and all he cared about was how the project went! She kept her temper with difficulty.

'The project went very well,' she told him, trying to keep the rising emotion out of her voice. 'As far as I can tell, the ski-centre should be a great success.' She glanced at him as he nodded with satisfaction, pausing as she tried to read his devious mind. 'What about me, Uncle?' she asked quietly. 'What about my debt? Can I assume it is cleared now?'

He frowned, taking the cigar out of his mouth and tapping it thoughtfully on the edge of the ashtray. 'Ah—I'm afraid not quite, my dear. You see, from what I gather you haven't succeeded in captivating Adam completely, have you? Bobby isn't here now, but I'm very much afraid it will be as you yourself predicted. I daresay that the moment they are together again she and Adam will take up where they left off.' He stroked his beard. 'Absence makes the heart grow fonder, as you no doubt know from your fiance's reaction. To say it's irritating is putting it mildly!'

She was appalled. 'I don't understand,' she said. 'If you thought that would happen why did you tell John where I was? You can hardly blame me if your plan didn't work!' But even while she was saying it she knew she had been used. He had simply been stringing her along—using her to keep Adam in Switzerland for a few days longer than he would normally have stayed for some reason best known to himself.

'Are you telling me that you're forcing me into bankruptcy after all?' she asked bleakly.

He blew out a cloud of smoke and smiled benignly at her through it. 'My dear Danielle! What do you take me for? Of course I won't see my only brother's daughter in the bankruptcy courts. I intend to take this place over and adopt Adam's plan for it. As for poor Matthew's debt. As you insisted on paying it off I shall allow you as much time as you like to do so, naturally. And of course we can take the furniture and fittings of the hotel into consideration, even though I shall have to get rid of most of them.'

She stared down at her plate, desperation chilling her heart. Where was she to go and how on earth was she to repay the debt? 'Thank you.' She looked up at him, one last faint hope rising forlornly in her mind. 'Would there be a job for me here at The Royalty?' she asked.

He shook his head slowly. 'I'm afraid I can't see that working very well.' He flicked the ash from his cigar. 'No—better if you got a job and became independent. For one thing, Adam will be here for some time and you'd hardly feel comfortable with him now, would you? And for another, we wouldn't want the staff to feel they were trying to work for two masters. There is bound to be a conflict of loyalties and I'm sure that you want them all to keep *their* jobs.'

So that was it, she thought bitterly. It was blackmail all the way. 'I see,' she said. 'I assume you'll give me time to find somewhere else to live?'

'Of course. Take as much time as you need, my dear.' he told her magnanimously. 'And I do hope you'll keep in close touch.'

What he really meant of course, was: 'Don't lose sight of the fact that you are still in my debt!'

There was only one person she could turn to and she rang him that evening—only to be told that he was out. Arthur's friend, Patrick Dench, told her that he was on the trail of something interesting, but would not tell her more.

'I know that Arthur will want to tell you about it himself,' he said. 'He'll be so sorry to have missed you. Look, why don't you pop round for coffee tomorrow morning? I'll be at work then and you can have the place to yourselves.' He gave her the address and she scribbled it down in her diary.

'Tell him I'll see him at about ten-thirty,' she told him.

*　　　*　　　*

155

It was wonderful to see Arthur again. He looked fit and well and there was an air of suppressed excitement about him as he opened the door of Patrick Dench's little cottage and welcomed her in.

'Danny! Come in, love. I've been so worried about you, dashing off to Switzerland like that. You must tell me all about it over coffee. I got up early this morning and made some of your favourite Danish pastries.'

She followed him through to the sunny little sitting room where he had already laid a dainty tray and had the coffee already 'perking' in the electric percolator. As he pulled up a comfortable chair for her he peered at her carefully for the first time and his eyes clouded.

'Danny—there *is* something wrong, isn't there? Don't try to tell me there isn't. I've known that little face too long not to recognise the signs.' He poured a cup of hot, strong coffee and passed it to her. 'Want to tell me about it?'

His kindness was the last straw and she struggled to control the lump in her throat, taking a sip of her coffee in the hope that it would steady her. But when she looked up at Arthur's homely face, wrinkled with anxiety for her, and felt the touch of his fatherly hand on her arm it was too much. Putting her cup down on the table she dissolved helplessly into tears and once she had started she couldn't seem to stop. The tears cascaded down her cheeks as she fumbled vainly in her bag for a handkerchief. Arthur silently produced a large, outsized one and moved onto the arm of her chair to cradle her head against his chest. He didn't press her for an explanation but as soon as her sobs had subsided enough for her to find her voice she began, pouring out the story to him bit by bit. She kept nothing back, knowing that, having come this far, it was useless to try to pull the wool over Arthur's eyes about her true feelings.

'I'm in love with him, Arthur,' she told him huskily. 'It's real and it hurts so much. I didn't know it was possible to feel as deeply as this. I know there can never be any other man for me and that's the awful part, because he must hate me now. He must think I was acting—doing what Uncle James sent me there to do.' She glanced up at him. 'I know it must be hard for you to understand. I don't expect you to think kindly of Adam after what he did to you.'

But Arthur shook his head. 'On the contrary, I'm very grateful to him. He brought me to my senses—gave me that push I badly needed and as it happens it couldn't have worked out better—but I'll tell you about that later.' He took her hand and squeezed it warmly. 'I was wrong that afternoon, Danny. Full of self-pity. I should have been thinking of you, not myself. *He* told me that.' He smiled wryly. 'That's one of the few things I

157

remember!'

She looked up at him, her heart twisting painfully. 'He said that?'

Arthur nodded. 'He did—and a lot more besides. I got the distinct impression that he admired you a great deal. He made me feel very ashamed of myself, even in the condition I was in at the time. And at least he put me into a taxi—didn't cast me adrift as it were.'

'I didn't know any of this.' She smiled reminiscently in spite of her distress, recalling the occasion. 'He cooked dinner himself that evening. He made me help. He had everyone running round in circles but he made a marvellous job of it ...' Her voice caught as the tears began afresh. 'Oh, Arthur—it could have been so wonderful and now—now it's all spoilt!'

Arthur cleared his throat noisily. 'Don't cry like that Danny, love. You'll have me at it in a minute, I wish to heaven you'd come to me before you fell in with your uncle's plan. Obviously you realise now how silly and dangerous it was.' He patted her shoulder. 'But it's not going to help, going back over that ground now. You've more practical problems to face. We'd better make some kind of plan. Where are you going to live? Do you have a job in mind at all?'

With an effort she pulled herself together and looked at him. 'No. All I know at the moment is that I have to get out of The

Royalty as soon as I can. For one thing, Uncle James has more or less told me to go and for another, Adam will be back from Switzerland any day and I can't face him at the moment—perhaps not ever!'

Arthur nodded, looking at her thoughtfully. 'I think the time has come to tell you about my plans. I'm going to open a little restaurant. I've found just the place and I can move in when I like—so how about you coming to live and work with me?'

She stared at him in surprise. 'Arthur! I don't know what to say.'

He smiled. 'Don't expect wonders. All I can promise is lots of back-breaking hard work! The place used to be a wine merchant's. There's a furnished flat above with two bedrooms and plenty of space. That's no problem. But downstairs needs completely renovating before I can open as an eating place. There'll be furniture and equipment to buy, the licence to apply for—advertising to plan—everything.'

Danielle swallowed hard. 'It sounds fun, Arthur—I'd love it.' She bit her lip. 'But I couldn't put any cash into it. I'm afraid I still owe Uncle James a lot and I'm determined to pay back every penny.'

Arthur shook his head at her. 'I wouldn't dream of taking any money from you after all your father did for me!' He leaned forward, his face alight with enthusiasm. 'Listen. All these years I've had nothing to spend my salary on.' He grinned wryly. 'Except the odd bottle of whisky, but that's all over now! I'm not short of cash—but I *am* short of reliable help and good company. So how about it?'

'When do we start?' she asked him, cheering up.

He spread his hands. 'I signed the lease yesterday. The place is mine and the flat is quite habitable. We could move in today if you wanted to get away quickly.'

'Oh, Arthur, *could* we?'

He grinned. 'How about three-thirty this afternoon?'

Danielle threw her arms around his neck and hugged him hard. 'Arthur, you're an angel! You've just saved my life!'

Arthur blew his nose hard and made a great show of finding a pencil and scrap of paper. 'Here's the address.' He pressed the paper into her hand. 'I'll meet you there.'

Danielle had plenty to think about as she drove back towards The Royalty, the least of which was how she could raise some money quickly so as to start paying her uncle off. Suddenly she realised that one answer was right there in her hands. On impulse, she steered the car onto the forecourt of the first garage she saw.

The car salesman went over the car carefully and after asking her for proof of her identity and the relevant documents, offered

160

her a fair price. The next thing she knew she was standing at the bus stop, feeling rather dazed, with the cheque in her handbag. Maybe it was only about one quarter of what she owed, but at least it was a start.

Packing to leave was a painful business and Danielle found herself wishing it was all behind her as she looked around the room that had been hers for so long.

Her uncle had been taken aback when she had handed him the cheque and told him she would be leaving that afternoon. No doubt he was wondering how she had managed to raise so much money and find a job and accommodation so quickly. She decided not to satisfy his curiosity. As she was packing her few pieces of jewellery she fingered the diamond pendant, toying with the idea of selling that too, but she put the idea firmly from her, pushing the tiny box into a corner of her handbag. She had precious little to remind her of the happy times she and her father had spent together. She would not part with his special gift to her.

She was snapping her case shut—taking one last look round the room, when suddenly the telephone on her bedside table rang. She picked it up.

'Hello?'

'Miss Denver, it's Sandra. Mr Peterson is here. He rang several times while you were out. He wants to see you. May he come up?'

'No! Tell him I'm just coming down. And order a taxi for me, will you, Sandra?' She lowered her voice. 'What does Mr Peterson want? Did he say?'

Obviously John was standing nearby and Sandra answered in a strained whisper: 'I believe he has brought your suitcase, Miss Denver. The one you left in his car yesterday.'

'Oh—of course.' Danielle bit her lip. Damn! He would arrive just at this moment. Another few minutes and she would have left.

She steeled herself to the fact that she would have to see him and go through the tedious business of explaining why she was leaving. 'I'll be right down, Sandra,' she said firmly. 'Will you send one of the porters up for my luggage, please?'

John was waiting by the reception desk, her cream leather suitcase at his side. He looked curiously at the luggage the porter deposited by the door.

'What's going on?' he asked.

'I'm leaving,' she told him. 'The Denver Group is taking over and there's no place for me here. I have another job to go to.'

He turned to the porter. 'You can put Miss Denver's luggage in my car, Peter. What won't fit into the boot can go on the roof rack. Cancel that taxi, Sandra. I'll take Miss Denver wherever it is she's going!'

Danielle opened her mouth to protest but he was already halfway through the door, carrying her two smallest cases. She sighed resignedly as she handed her key to Sandra along with an envelope.

'My new address is in there, Sandra. You'll send on any letters that come, won't you?'

'Of course.' The girl's eyes were misty as she said: 'You will keep in touch, won't you, Miss Denver? Everyone thinks it's awful, you having to go like this. We'd all rather work for you than anyone else.'

Danielle forced a smile. 'Of course I'll keep in touch. I'll let you into a secret—Arthur is opening a new restaurant and I'm going to help him with it. But keep it to yourself for the time being, eh?'

The girl nodded, her eyes brightening. 'Oh, that's lovely! I'm so glad.'

'I'm ready when you are, Danielle.' John stood in the doorway, looking impatient.

'I'm coming.' She stood in the hall, taking a last look round. It was hard to accept the fact that this was no longer her home—that soon it would be unrecognisable to her. With a sigh and a last wistful smile at Sandra, she turned and followed John reluctantly out onto the forecourt.

The moment the car moved away he asked the inevitable question: 'Where is your own car?'

She sighed. 'I've sold it, if you must know.'

He turned to stare at her. 'Sold it! Why?'

'Because I need every penny I can scrape

together to pay off my father's debt,' she said wearily. 'I would have thought you'd have worked that out for yourself.'

'You should have asked me,' he admonished. 'I expect you got some ridiculously low price for it. What makes you do these impulsive things, Danielle? And by the way, where are you going and what's this job you've found?'

Briefly she explained Arthur's plan to him, watching his doubtful expression with irritation.

'I'm really looking forward to it,' she told him with forced enthusiasm. 'It will be enormous fun—a challenge! Anyway I have to have a job and a roof over my head, don't I?'

'You could have moved into Langworth House,' he told her. 'After all, we'll be married soon and then Arthur will have to manage without you. We could even move the date forward—get a special licence . . .'

She sighed, biting her lip in an effort not to shout at him. 'I've *told* you, John. I can't marry you. It's over.'

'You'll get over that feeling. It's pre-wedding nerves,' he said smugly. 'I'm told that all brides get these irrational doubts—*Hell and damnation!*' He swung the wheel of the car over, mounting the grass verge to avoid a car that swept at speed round the curve in the drive. 'Blast the man! Driving like a maniac! I should report him to the police. Did you see

164

who it was?' He turned to Danielle and his expression changed as he registered the shock on her face. 'What's the matter? You've gone as white as a sheet.'

But it was not the near-collision that had shaken her. It was the driver of the car, glimpsed through the tinted windscreen of the Mercedes as it had swung past them. He had seen her too. Their eyes had locked briefly as he passed—and there could be no doubt that he had recognised the car as John's—and noticed her luggage piled on the roof rack. Deep inside, her heart ached at the anger and bitterness she had read in his eyes.

'Adam—oh, *Adam!*' she cried silently, her heart breaking.

CHAPTER NINE

The weeks that followed were hectic for Danielle and Arthur. A date was set for the opening of the restaurant, which Arthur had decided was to be called 'Danni's', and to be ready they threw themselves into a frenzy of preparation. The licence was applied for and Arthur set about the business of buying his kitchen equipment while Danielle organised and designed the decor of the little restaurant. Builders and decorators moved in with all the necessary paraphernalia and work began.

The stock of wines was carefully selected by Arthur the moment he knew that the licence had been granted and a large freezer was installed in the storeroom off the kitchen, its contents growing daily as Arthur happily cooked in his gleaming new kitchen.

Danielle made herself as busy as she could, arranging for eye-catching advertisements to be inserted in all the local papers as well as the county magazines. Upstairs in the flat she made the place as homely as she could with personal possessions they had both brought with them from The Royalty. She tried hard to blot out her unhappiness with hard work. Some of the time it worked—but mostly it didn't.

Late at night when the rest of the world was asleep she lay staring into the darkness, longing for the sight of Adam's face, aching for his touch and the sound of his voice till the pain inside her grew almost too much to bear.

While they were so busy she had managed to keep John at arms' length. He rang her frequently and took to dropping in in the evenings, but the flat was too small for them to be alone together for more than a few minutes and somehow the serious talking that became increasingly necessary between them never happened. Danielle put the problem to the back of her mind, too weary and dispirited to tackle John's persistence. Although she had made it as clear as she knew how that marriage between them was out of the question, he was still behaving as though their engagement was on, his attitude being that everything would be fine once they were safely married. She had given up trying in the end; putting off the final showdown and promising herself that once the restaurant was open and running she would have it out with him once and for all.

It was a few days before the opening when Danielle was surprised one morning by a telephone call. At first she didn't recognise the voice.

'Good morning, is that Danni's restaurant?'

'That's right. Can I help you?'

'Is that Miss Denver—Danielle?'

'Speaking.'

'It's Bobby Hayward, Danielle. Adam was wondering if you could come over to The Royalty this afternoon—say about two-thirty?'

Danielle's heart turned a somersault at the mention of his name. 'No, I don't think there's anything to be gained by meeting.'

'It's important,' Bobby told her. '*Very* important, both that you come *and* that it is this afternoon. If you've something else on perhaps you could rearrange it.'

'What is it about?' Danielle asked guardedly. 'And how—how did you know where to find me?'

The other girl laughed. 'There's a double page spread in this month's *Cotswold Trumpet*. I thought you were probably responsible for placing it.'

Danielle bit her lip. How stupid the girl must think her. 'Oh—of course. I'd forgotten.'

'Can I tell him to expect you then?'

'You still haven't told me what it's about. As you can imagine, we're very busy at the moment and . . .'

'*Just be here*, Danielle. It's urgent!' Her heart almost stopped as Adam's voice cut into her faltering excuses. He must have been listening on an extension. Why couldn't he have spoken to her himself—told her what it was he wanted to see her about? She was about to ask him when there was a click and the line went dead. She put down the receiver with an exclamation of annoyance, making Arthur look up at her in surprise.

'What is it, Danny—not the agency, I hope?'

She shook her head. 'I was just about to tell him we're interviewing waitresses this afternoon.'

Arthur, who was reading the morning's batch of letters, looked at her over the tops of his reading glasses, raising an eyebrow at her. 'About to tell who?'

'Adam Scott!' Her voice shook slightly and she got up and walked over to the window, so that he shouldn't see the tell-tale colour in her cheeks. 'He asks—*demands* that I go over to The Royalty this afternoon—only *this* afternoon will do. Would you believe that anyone could be so arrogant? He must think I

168

have nothing better to do!'

Arthur took off his glasses and laid them down on the table. 'Maybe it's important. It sounds as though it is,' he told her calmly. 'Perhaps you'd be wise to do as he asks.'

'But I can't leave you with everything,' she protested. She turned and caught sight of his face. It was hopeless to try to pretend with Arthur. Her shoulders slumping, she asked: 'Oh, Arthur—what do you think he wants?'

'Come and sit down. Have another cup of coffee and calm down.' He poured it out for her. 'Maybe he wants to hear your side of the story. You want to have the chance to tell him, don't you?'

But Danielle shook her head. 'He's had weeks to ask me if he wanted to hear that. No. He's made up his mind about why I went to Switzerland. Anyway, I don't think it meant all that much to him.' She straightened her back and looked at Arthur in a brave attempt to convince him—and herself. 'I'm resigned to it now, anyway. It doesn't hurt any more.'

He gave her his wry, lop-sided smile. 'Oh come off it, Danny, love. You don't have to put on a show for me. Those eyes of yours speak volumes, you know. You don't have to tell me what you've been going through for the past few weeks. Look—I can manage the interviewing this afternoon perfectly well if you want to go. Do you?'

She sighed. 'Well . . .'

'Well, I think you should,' he told her decisively. 'It might not be anything personal at all. It could be something to do with your father's affairs. After all, you're not finished with all that yet, are you? I really don't think you can refuse to go.'

Privately Danielle felt that if it had been business Adam would have said so—or got Bobby to say so on the telephone. And if that were the case, why the need for her to go today? But she didn't voice her doubts. Instead she smiled at Arthur.

'Well—maybe you're right. Perhaps I'd better go.' She began to clear the table but Arthur's hand caught her wrist.

'Danny. Sit down a minute. Now that we're talking, there's something I want to say to you.'

She did as he said, wondering what it could be that made him look so grave.

'What are you going to do about John Peterson?' he asked. 'Maybe it's none of my business, but it seems to me that you're ducking the issue. If you're not going to marry him, shouldn't you tell him so once and for all?'

Danielle sighed. 'I've *tried*, Arthur. He just won't listen!'

'I think you know that you've got to *make* him listen, Danny,' Arthur said, his face concerned. 'It's a problem that won't just go away by ignoring it. John probably thinks you're young and need time to make up your mind. Maybe he thinks the Swiss episode was a sort of last fling that you needed before settling down. You've got to make him see that it was more than that.'

Danielle groaned. He was only echoing the thoughts she had been pushing to the back of her mind for weeks. 'I know, Arthur. It isn't easy though, convincing John.'

Arthur shook his head. 'Maybe that's another thing you should get down to today. Why not take some time off? Make it a day for tying up loose ends, eh?'

She took his advice. After an early lunch of sandwiches and coffee she took the small van Arthur had bought and drove over to Kingswood, trying not to feel too apprehensive about the coming interview.

As she drove round the curve in the drive and the house came into sight a sharp pang of nostalgia gripped her heart. It looked as though work was already underway on it. Workmen's vehicles stood on the forecourt and she could see white dust-sheets through some of the ground floor windows.

As she walked in through the front entrance Sandra looked up from the reception desk, smiling with pleasure. 'Miss Denver! How lovely to see you. Miss Hayward said you were coming this afternoon. I'll just ring through to the office . . .'

'That won't be necessary, Sandra.'

Danielle spun round, her heart jumping at

the sound of Adam's voice. He must have watched her arrival from the office window and now he stood framed in the office doorway, his eyes enigmatic as they looked unsmilingly into hers.

'Come into the office.' He turned and walked in, holding the door for her to follow. Sandra reached for the house phone.

'Shall I ring through to the kitchen for some tea?'

Danielle shook her head, smiling wryly at the girl. 'Don't bother, Sandra. I've a feeling this isn't going to take very long.'

The office had been redecorated. The pretty wallpaper Danielle had chosen was gone, replaced by plain walls, now almost covered in graphs and charts, maps and 'Denver Hotels' posters. A large computer had been installed and on the smart new desk in the window, which she took to be Adam's, was an imposing line up of telephones in various colours.

As Adam closed the door she looked at him. It seemed an age since she had seen him and her heart lurched. It was oddly surprising that all the little things she remembered so well about him were still there. The way he held his head; the movement of the strong, well manicured hands. Her heart twisted sickeningly as she felt a surge of longing for the touch of those hands. She studied his face as he seated himself at the desk, noticing the tiny lines at the corners of his mouth; trying to make up her mind whether or not they had deepened. She noticed that his hair was slightly longer than usual and wondered almost detachedly if he had been too busy to have it cut.

When he spoke to her she didn't register what he was saying for a moment and he had to repeat it. His tone was cool and impersonal. He might have been interviewing a prospective employee as he indicated a chair.

'I said, please sit down, Danielle. I appreciate that you're busy and I won't keep you long.'

'Thank you.' She sat uneasily on the edge of the chair, wondering what he was about to say to her.

Adam looked at her gravely. She felt as though the whole thing was some bizarre dream. An outsider, looking at them now, could well have taken them for strangers yet her mind was alive with memories that refused to be banished.

'I'll come straight to the point,' he said, crisply. 'I understand that you are trying to pay back an enormous debt owed to your uncle by your father.'

She started, jerked rudely back to cold reality. 'Who told you that?' Then she bit her lip, remembering John's outburst in the hotel bedroom in Switzerland.

Adam appeared not to notice her discomfort. 'I asked you to come here today specifically because your uncle is away in London at the moment. What I am about to say is strictly between ourselves and off the record. Do you understand, Danielle?'

She nodded, her mouth dry.

'It's this: My advice to you is to call his bluff. Tell him to sue you for it,' he told her bluntly.

She gave an ironic little laugh. 'Don't you think I have enough expense without that? Men like Uncle James always win, don't they?'

He leaned forward, his eyes snapping impatiently. 'If you can't trust me consult a solicitor. But do it quickly, before it's too late. I understand you've already paid back some of the money—and sold your car to do so.'

Where was he getting all this information about her, she wondered uneasily? 'Look— who told you about that?' she demanded. 'I think I have a right to know!'

He sighed. 'All right. I don't suppose it's any secret. John Peterson came to see me and . . .'

She sprang to her feet, her heart beating wildly. 'You've been discussing me with John? How dare you? How dare *he*?'

He looked suddenly tired as he waved a hand at her. 'Please, Danielle—sit down and hear me out.' He went on, slowly, as though he were weighing his words carefully. 'John was naturally troubled about you, as any fiance would be. I think I was able to settle his mind on one or two matters but when he brought up the matter of this debt again it made me think.

I've made a few discreet enquiries and I'm sure you'll find that you don't have to pay James anything.'

The significance of his last sentence was totally lost on her. What had he meant by: *I was able to settle his mind on one or two matters*? She could guess! He must have assured John that there was nothing serious between them—that the affair in Switzerland had been a put-up job; something her uncle had pressed her into doing against her will. The fact that it was partly true didn't help, but what neither of them seemed to care about was the way her emotions—her whole life, had been torn apart by it.

'Are you all right, Danielle? Do you understand what I'm trying to tell you?' He was looking intently at her white face. With an effort she dragged her thoughts back into line, forcing herself to concentrate on what he was trying to tell her.

'Yes—I'm all right. As to what you've been saying about Uncle James, I'm not so sure.'

'Do as I say,' he repeated. 'Call his bluff. James won't press you for the money, I promise you that. After all, he hasn't done so badly out of it. He's got The Royalty.'

She shook her head, still doubtful.

He got up and came round the desk to sit on one corner of it. Stroking his chin he looked at her thoughtfully for a moment. 'You're obviously going to need convincing and I can't say I blame you. I shouldn't be telling you this, Danielle,' he said slowly, 'but I happen to know that James has his eye on next year's Honours List. It wouldn't do much for his image if it got into the papers, would it?— *Hotel tycoon presses penniless niece for father's gambling debt.*' He looked at her, one eyebrow raised. 'See what I mean?'

She looked at him for a long moment, trying to read what was in his eyes. 'Why are you telling me all this, Adam?' she asked quietly.

His face clouded and he stood up, walking across to the window. There was a long pause before he said: 'Let's say I hate shady dealings, Danielle—people having the power to manipulate others for their own gain. I couldn't stand by and watch that sort of injustice.'

She frowned. 'But why should Uncle James do this to me?'

He shrugged. 'Something to do with old scores, maybe, rather than old debts. Perhaps there was more bad blood between him and your father than you realised.'

She got slowly to her feet, suddenly wanting to be gone from here. Anything that ever existed between Adam and herself was quite clearly dead as far as he was concerned and being in the same room with him, talking like this, was becoming more and more unbearable as the minutes passed. 'So what do you suggest I do?' she asked.

'Nothing.' He turned to look at her, his eyes dispassionate. 'Go home and forget it. If he has the nerve to ask for more money suggest that the newspapers might be interested in your story. Those are tactics he understands. Then I suggest that you marry John Peterson and settle down to your new venture. Make a new start.'

She was devastated. He might have been advising a casual acquaintance—at best, an employee. If she had wanted confirmation here it was. Clearly Adam cared no more for her than for a member of his staff. He was concerned about an injustice he felt she had been dealt and nothing more. She took a deep breath and began to gather up her bag and gloves.

'Thank you for—for going to so much trouble on my behalf. I'll certainly think about what you've said.' Her voice was tight with control. She looked at her watch. 'I'd better be going now. There's a lot to do.'

He smiled bleakly. 'I understand you're opening on Friday. May I wish you both the best of luck?'

She forced herself to return his smile. 'Thank you. Arthur has worked very hard. He deserves to succeed and he will if I have anything to do with it.'

Adam reached the door first and opened it for her. 'Goodbye, Danielle. I hope things go well for you,' he told her quietly.

She thanked him, the tears gathering painfully in her throat. It all felt so final. As he opened the door for her she had the curious feeling that he was letting her out of his life.

She drove away from The Royalty as fast as she could, not stopping until she was well out of sight of the place; then she turned the van into a quiet little lane, switched off the engine and laid her head on her arms, giving way to the tears she had held back so long, sobbing as though her heart would break.

At last there were no more tears. Danielle dried her eyes, feeling exhausted yet relieved at the release of tension. She sat back, making an effort to clear her mind, forcing herself to think things through logically. What Adam had told her about her father's debt was an enormous relief. As to his advice about marrying John, it only underlined for her what Arthur said this morning. She must talk to him today. Only then would she feel free to make that new start Adam had spoken of.

She rang John at the office, using a callbox. He sounded surprised to hear from her.

'Of course we can meet, Danielle. I'll pick you up about seven-thirty this evening. We'll go out to dinner.'

'Can't we meet now, John?' she asked. 'I have something important to talk to you about.'

'No. I'm tied up all afternoon,' he told her. 'And I have someone with me at the moment, so I can't talk now.'

John seemed in a good mood when he called to pick her up that evening. He told her he had booked a table at The Swan, a beautiful seventeenth-century inn on the banks of the Avon.

As they drove she told him she had been to The Royalty that afternoon at Adam's request, explaining to him what she had learned from the meeting, John nodded.

'Just as I thought.' He turned to look at her. 'Now perhaps you can see why you should have asked me before haring off to Switzerland on that mad errand. Perhaps you can understand why I questioned your motives. It seemed to me incredible that anyone could do such a thing unless they actually wanted to.' He reached out to pat her knee. 'But Scott reassured me on that count when I went to see him about your father's debt.'

'So good of you both to clear my name,' she said dryly. 'I suppose it didn't occur to you to ask me before you discussed it with him?'

He looked at her coolly. 'Is this what you wanted to speak to me about, Danielle? Are you piqued because Scott and I have been talking about you?'

She shook her head. 'Yes—but we'll get to that later.'

In the pretty powder room at The Swan she took her time, studying her face in the mirror as she combed her hair and applied more lipstick. She wished the evening could be over. Although she was convinced that she and John were wrong for each other, she hated the prospect of having to convince him. He seemed so sure of her, so positive that he knew her mind better than she did. It wouldn't be easy making him understand that marriage between them was out of the question.

In the bar he was waiting for her, a dry sherry already ordered, and she wondered fleetingly if he would ever learn how irritating it was to have one's wants anticipated.

'John—there's something I have to say to you,' she began, but he waved a hand at her as a waiter came to show them to their table.

It was as they were settling themselves at the table that she saw them. At a table on the terrace, on the other side of the long windows, sitting in the evening sunshine—Adam and Bobby Hayward, their heads together over drinks. Danielle hid her face behind the menu, her heart turning to stone, but John had already seen the colour drain from her face.

'What is it? You look as though you've seen a ghost.' He followed her gaze. 'Oh, it's them—Scott and his P.A. I saw them while I was waiting for you, but they seemed too engrossed in each other to notice me. Now— what will you have?' He studied the menu for a moment, then looked at her. 'Danielle! I said what will you have!'

180

She shook her head at him, her lip quivering. Panic seized her as she realised she was about to make a fool of herself. Blindly, she got to her feet. 'It's—no use, John,' she whispered, hastily gathering up her handbag. 'I—I can't stay here. I'm sorry.' Knees trembling, she made her way blindly through the tables, hardly able to see where she was going for the tears that blurred her vision; knowing or caring little for the curious eyes that followed her progress.

CHAPTER TEN

Danielle fled to the comparative privacy of the powder room and did her best to control the feeling of faintness that threatened to overwhelm her. Would it always be like this, she wondered despairingly? How long would it be before she could forget him—how long before the unbearable hurt would lessen?

John was waiting in the car when she joined him fifteen minutes later. Slipping into the seat beside him she mumbled her apology:

'I'm sorry I spoiled your evening, John. I couldn't help it. You see . . .'

'I know,' he interrupted, his face resigned. 'You needn't explain, it's all right.' He turned to look at her. 'I saw your face—the effect seeing him had on you. I'd be a fool if I didn't

181

acknowledge that I'm fighting a losing battle. You really *are* in love with him, aren't you? That's what this evening was all about. You wanted to finish it—once and for all.'

She turned a stricken face to him. 'I *tried* to tell you a dozen times, John, but you wouldn't listen. I'm sorry.' She held out her engagement ring. 'Please, John—take it.'

He accepted the ring in silence, pocketing it thoughtfully, then he said: 'So it wasn't an act—what happened in Switzerland?'

She sighed. 'Uncle James presented me with a *fait accompli*, but I couldn't even have considered agreeing to it if I hadn't already been in love with Adam. I suppose deep down I must have known that all along.' She lifted her shoulders. 'But it doesn't matter now anyway. If it's any consolation it's all on one side. Adam doesn't share my feelings, as you must have gathered. I wouldn't blame you for thinking it served me right.'

He glanced at her. 'You're quite sure— about us I mean? You wouldn't like to cool things for a while and then try again?'

She shook her head. 'It wouldn't be any use, John—not now. It wouldn't be fair to you.'

He switched on the ignition and urged the car towards the carpark exit. 'I see,' he said resignedly. 'Well—that's that, I suppose.'

That night she wept long into the small hours; silent, hopeless tears that brought her no comfort—for John; for herself—but most

182

of all, at the searing memory of those two heads, seen so close together on the terrace of The Swan. Adam's and Bobby's. Clearly they were as close as ever and it hurt as nothing had ever hurt before.

*　　　*　　　*

By Friday morning 'Danni's' was fully booked for the opening evening and Arthur was in a high state of excitement. When Danielle got up at seven he had already been in the kitchen for hours, baking rolls and doing as much advance work as he could, ready for the great event. To mark the occasion there was to be free wine for everyone as well as a red rose for each of the ladies. For Arthur it was the most important day of his life.

They worked hard all morning, breaking for lunch at twelve on Danielle's insistence.

'This simply won't do, Arthur,' she scolded him. 'You look tired already. At this rate you'll be worn out before the evening begins!'

After lunch she made him go upstairs for a short rest while she busied herself arranging the flowers for the restaurant. She heard him come down at about half-past three and begin pottering about in the kitchen, checking on the large pans of soup that were simmering on the stove and the roasts already cooking in the ovens.

She was just putting the finishing touches to

the tables when it happened. There was a loud crash, followed by a scream of pain. She ran into the kitchen and froze with horror at the sight that confronted her. Arthur was leaning on the table, his face contorted with pain, whilst the floor was awash with boiling soup from an overturned pan.

'Arthur! My God! What happened?' She pressed him into a chair and began to roll up his sleeve but he let out a yell of agony and shot out his other hand to stop her.

'No—leave it!' Tears of agony filled his eyes as he grabbed a teatowel and wrapped it round the scalded arm and hand. 'I was reaching up to the cupboard,' he told her between clenched teeth. 'I caught the pan with my elbow. I—I think I need a doctor, Danny.'

'I'll get the van out,' she told him. 'I'll take you straight to the hospital. Try not to worry.'

'Not the hospital!' he protested. 'They might keep me in and there's the opening!'

She brushed his protests aside. 'First things first. Got to get that arm attended to before we do anything else!'

It was an hour later that she left the hospital. Arthur had sustained second-degree burns and shock. As he had feared, he was being kept in overnight just to make sure there were no complications. She had been allowed to see him and tried to reassure him that everything would be all right. Luckily he was too heavily sedated to worry much.

As she walked to the van her mind spun. Just three short hours from now 'Danni's' was due to open, with its owner and chef laid up in a hospital bed and her own culinary accomplishments strictly limited.

Back at the flat she made herself a strong cup of coffee and tried to force herself to think constructively. Ten minutes later she was dialling the number of The Royalty. They were closed for alterations. The new chef there would surely come over and help her out for tonight.

Sandra listened to Danielle's bad news and plea for help with dismay.

'Oh, Miss Denver. If only I could help. You see the kitchen staff are all on holiday this week—while the kitchens are being redecorated and equipped. There's only me and the upstairs staff. If I can do anything . . .'

Danielle sighed. 'No. I'm in desperate need of an expert chef. Never mind, Sandra. It can't be helped. I'll get onto the agency. I'll ring off now. I must get them before they close.'

She dialled the number several times but found it engaged. At last, anxious not to delay any longer, she pulled on a coat and ran out to the garage to get the van out again. She would go round in person.

She had known Miss Maples at the agency for years. The small, elderly woman looked at her with concern, fluttering her hands agitatedly. 'Oh, Miss Denver, I'm sorry. I've absolutely no one I can offer you at the moment.'

Danielle's shoulders slumped with despair. 'Oh, no! That's it then. You were my last hope.' There was nothing for it now but to cancel the opening. Her mind ran feverishly ahead. She would have to get back to the restaurant as quickly as she could—ring everyone she had a number for. As for the rest, she would just have to explain to them when they arrived and pray for their understanding. She smiled at Miss Maples. 'Thanks anyway. I know you would have helped if you could.'

She drove back to 'Danni's' through the build-up of late afternoon traffic, biting her lip in anguish and frustration at the speed with which she was forced to travel. Every set of traffic lights seemed to be against her and the queues stretched endlessly. Tomorrow, when Arthur recovered from the medication, he was going to be devastated at the ruination of the day he had worked so hard for. Sometimes it seemed there was no justice in life. If only she could rid herself of the feeling that she had let him down.

Putting the van away, she felt in her pocket for her key and realised with a stab of dismay that in her haste to get to the agency she had left the place unlocked, but remembering the greasy mess of spilled soup still congealing on the kitchen floor she reflected wryly that any burglar would surely have changed his mind quickly at the prospect of wading through that!

But when she opened the door a spotless floor met her astonished eyes. Everything was spick-and-span. Pans were bubbling on the stove and the kitchen looked businesslike again. She was still standing on the threshold, a dazed expression on her face when a voice behind her commanded:

'What kept you? The waitresses have already begun to arrive! Well, don't just stand there! Get that coat off and make a start. We've got a restaurant full of customers to feed in just under an hour!' She found herself looking up at a tall, white clad figure, imposing in Arthur's tall chef's hat. Her heart almost burst with relief.

'*Adam*! How did you know . . . ?'

He took her arm and drew her into the kitchen, thrusting an apron into her hands. 'Never mind all that. I'm here, that's all that matters! If we work flat out we might still make it on time for your first booking!'

There was no time for further explanations. Adam had already taken control of the staff and Danielle was grateful for it as she set about carrying out her own routine, relieved beyond belief that 'Danni's' would be opening after all.

*   *   *

187

It was after midnight when Danielle saw the last satisfied customer off the premises and locked up securely. In the kitchen the last of the kitchen staff were leaving. As the two women left, calling out their goodnights, Danielle and Adam faced each other across the kitchen; alone for the first time since he had arrived. She felt her heartbeat quicken as she looked at him. It was the moment she had dreaded all evening. It had been one mad rush ever since he had arrived. There had been no time for questions; she had hardly seen him except on her few brief forays into the kitchen. Now they faced each other; now she could ask all the questions she wanted. But suddenly she found herself tongue-tied and at a loss for words. She felt herself beginning to panic, her stomach churning with apprehension. Any moment now he would say goodnight and walk out through the door. She couldn't—*mustn't*, let that happen. But what did she say—do?

He turned and smiled at her calmly, beginning to peel off his white overalls. 'Well, when you see Arthur I think you can safely tell him that you have a success on your hands.'

She smiled shakily. 'It's thanks entirely to you. Without your help tonight would have been a non-starter. I can't begin to thank you, Adam. But I still don't understand . . .'

'It's simple,' he interrupted. 'I was in Reception when you telephoned Sandra. I overheard everything you said.'

She frowned, shaking her head. 'But if you heard, you must have known I was on my way to the agency. For all you knew Miss Maple might have supplied someone ...' She stopped, her mouth dropping open at the smile on his face. 'It wasn't *you*? You surely didn't ... ?'

'Guilty, I'm afraid. I sabotaged it—fixed Miss Maple,' he confessed. 'I made her promise to say she hadn't anyone available. The poor old soul was horrified at first. I had my work cut out convincing her that I wasn't a spiteful rival but I managed it in the end!'

Danielle remembered the engaged telephone line and Miss Maple's agitated manner. It all fitted now. She looked at him, her heart drumming unevenly against her ribs. 'Why, Adam? Why did you do it?'

His eyes met hers levelly. 'It was too good to miss—the chance I'd been waiting for,' he said simply. He had stripped off the overalls to reveal jeans and tee-shirt. Slowly he crossed the kitchen till they stood facing each other. 'It suddenly occurred to me that this was where I came in, Danny,' he said quietly. 'The day when I sacked Arthur seemed to be the turning point for us. I'd half made up my mind that it was that incident that made you agree to your uncle's plan.'

She shook her head. 'Revenge? Nothing could be further from the truth.'

He shrugged. 'But you must admit that from

that day on things started to go wrong. So logically, it seemed a good place to step in and try to put them right.'

He was looking at her intently and her nerve suddenly failed her. She wasn't quite sure where the conversation was going and she was terribly afraid of saying something that would reveal the depth of her feelings. She looked at her watch. 'I—It's very late. You must be wanting to get back. I don't want to keep you. Bobby will be wondering where you are.' There was a moment's silence and she looked up to see a puzzled expression in his eyes.

'Bobby?'

'Yes. Won't she be waiting up for you?'

He shook his head perplexedly. 'Bobby is about five thousand miles away,' he told her, looking at his own watch. 'And at this moment she'll probably be getting ready to go out to dinner.' He laughed at her astonished expression. 'Bobby left a couple of days ago to take up a new job in New York. I took her out to dinner at The Swan a few nights ago as a goodbye gesture. We saw you and John there but when we came to look for you later, you'd gone. Bobby would have liked to say goodbye.'

Danielle felt the hot colour flood her cheeks. 'Oh!—I see,' she said softly.

He put his hands on her shoulders, shaking his head as he looked down at her. 'No you don't. There's an awful lot you don't see, Danielle.' He kissed her, gently at first, then as

190

she relaxed against him, he drew her close, his mouth claiming hers hungrily. As they drew apart he cupped her face, smoothing her cheekbones with his thumbs to find them wet with her tears. 'There's such a lot I want to tell you, darling,' he whispered. 'But it's so late and you're tired . . .'

She looked up at him, her eyes starry with tears, hardly daring to acknowledge the hope in her heart. 'I'm not at all tired,' she told him. 'We could have coffee—upstairs in the flat, where it's more comfortable.'

In the small living room above the restaurant Danielle poured coffee while Adam launched into his story: 'All that James told you about Bobby and me was pure fabrication,' he began. 'There wasn't—and never has, been anything between us, except that she was the best P.A. I've ever worked with. He used you to keep me out of the way because *he* intended to ask her to marry him.'

Danielle stared at him. 'Bobby and—and *Uncle James*? But she's young enough to be his daughter!'

'Precisely!' Adam smiled. '*And* to give him the son he'd always wanted—to be heir to the Denver Group when he finally gives up.'

Danielle shook her head. 'But—I thought *you* would be his heir.'

Adam gave her a wry smile. 'You weren't the only one! James married my mother for her money—money my father made by sheer

191

hard work. With my help he built the Denver Group on that money and made my mother's life hell into the bargain. I'll admit that I thought he owed me something on that score alone, but it seems I was wrong.' He lifted his shoulders. 'Bobby saw through it all and turned him down flat, by the way. For obvious reasons she felt she couldn't stay, so she handed in her notice as soon as I got back from Switzerland. James and I had a big showdown this morning. We've parted company for good.'

Danielle looked at him in dismay. 'Oh dear—I feel responsible for it all somehow.'

'You were in a way.' He smiled wryly at her. 'We seem to have wrought some pretty sweeping changes in each other's lives, don't we?' He picked up her ringless left hand. 'Like this for instance. Was I responsible for this?' His eyes met hers. '*Was* I, Danny?'

She nodded, her heart quickening. 'I think you know you were. John and I were never right for each other. But it took you to prove it to me.'

He pressed his lips into the palm, then held the hand against his cheek. 'I won't pretend I wasn't angry over what happened in Switzerland. But after I discovered the full truth that anger evaporated a little. I tried to put myself in your place—thought of all you'd laid on the line and the sacrifice you might have made to pay back that damned debt. That was why I spoke to John as I did—tried my best to patch things up for you.' He gave her a quirky grin. 'I'm not given to noble gestures and I don't mind admitting that it didn't come easily.'

She sighed, leaning her head against his shoulder. 'Oh, Adam. And all the time I thought you must hate me.'

He looked down at her. 'Hate you!' he smiled wryly. 'How much easier it would have been for me if I had! Why do you think I sent for you that day—tried to put you wise about James and his double dealing? I couldn't bear to stand by and see you ripped off.' He shook his head. 'You'll never know the struggle I had not to take you in my arms and kiss you that day.' He drew her close. 'Danny,' he whispered, his lips moving against her hair. 'You'll never know how much I regretted not making love to you that night in Switzerland. I wanted you so much and I've told myself a million times that I must have been raving mad! It was just that I wanted it to be perfect between us. To me it meant so much more than a mere affair. That was why I was so angry when I thought it meant so little to you.' She opened her mouth to say something but he stopped her, a finger against her lips as he looked down at her. 'Danielle—that night I stopped you from saying something. I said I'd ask you to say it to me again some day . . .' He cupped her chin, tipping her face upwards towards him. 'I'm asking you now.'

She looked into his eyes for a long moment. She seemed to have come such a long way—along a path strewn with pitfalls, doubts and heartache. Could it really be over? She moistened her lips and her voice trembled slightly as she said: 'I love you, Adam.' Then, because the phrase seemed so trite—the words so inadequate to describe all that she felt, she added: 'Now and tomorrow and—and always.'

His arms tightened round her and his lips claimed hers in a long searching kiss that left her in no doubt about his feelings for her. For a long time neither of them spoke, then Adam suddenly released her, holding her slightly away to look down at her. 'I almost forgot. I have a present for you!' He felt in his pocket for something, then took her hand and placed a small, cold object into it. Danielle looked at it, then up at him, a puzzled expression in her eyes.

'It's a key!'

He smiled. 'That's right. The key to The Royalty. During our showdown I managed to convince James that he owed me that. It was by way of being my severance pay.' He closed her fingers round it. 'And it's for you.'

Her eyes were incredulous as she looked at him. 'I don't believe it! I must be dreaming!'

He kissed her. 'You're not—and just to prove it, there's a real live snag to go with it.'

'Oh ...' The smile left her face as she

braced herself for what it might be. 'Don't tell me, I think I know—there's still a massive debt to pay?'

He shook his head, his eyes grave. 'No, not that. I hardly know how to tell you this, but you'll have to know sooner or later. After my split with James I find myself looking for a job.' He touched an imaginary forelock. 'So if you need a handy-man, Miss Denver—not to mention a partner . . .'

She burst into relieved laughter. 'Oh, Adam, you fool! Do you mean it? Would you really help me to run The Royalty?'

'Ah—now that rather depends on the terms you can offer me,' His eyes were serious as he looked down at her, though a spark of mischief twinkled in their depths. 'With my experience I come rather expensive.'

She looked up at him, her eyes dancing with happiness. 'Name your price!'

'You'd have to marry me, I'm afraid,' he told her gravely. 'I couldn't settle for anything less. I have my reputation to consider, you see.'

There was only one reply to that—and only one way in which to express it. Her heart full, Danielle slid her arms around his waist and laid her head against his chest. 'Give me one good reason why I should say yes,' she asked him softly.

He did!

Chivers Large Print Direct

If you have enjoyed this Large Print book and would like to build up your own collection of Large Print books and have them delivered direct to your door, please contact **Chivers Large Print Direct**.

Chivers Large Print Direct offers you a full service:

☆ **Created to support your local library**

☆ **Delivery direct to your door**

☆ **Easy-to-read type and attractively bound**

☆ **The very best authors**

☆ **Special low prices**

For further details either call Customer Services on 01225 443400 or write to us at

Chivers Large Print Direct
FREEPOST (BA 1686/1)
Bath
BA1 3QZ